FOR BLACK GIRLS

who have yet to forgive themselves

TLHALEFO TEFO MOLATLHEGI

African Perspectives Publishing
PO Box 95342, Grant Park 2051,
Johannesburg, South Africa
www.africanperspectives.co.za

ISBN PRINT: 978-1-990931-25-3
ISBN DIGITAL: 978-1-990931-31-4

Cover Image: Studio Studio
Editor: A Read Black Girl
Proof Reader: Rose Francis
Typesetting: Phumzile Mondlani

Contents

Dedication

This book, after years and years of creating, is dedicated to my mother, **Mosadiwapula Peggy Molatlhegi**, because she embodies blackness, womanhood and forgiveness.

My not-so-little sister, **Mokgabo Galeangwe Tlou**. For always reminding me how to love, and how to forgive myself and others.

My niece**, Oteng Boago-Jwa-Modimo Molatlhegi**, because one day, you too, will need to forgive yourself.

To **Maselelo Olivia Molatlhegi**. Thank you for your unconditional love.

Last, but not least, my grandmother, **Morati Girley Molatlhegi**, who is my ancestor and spiritual warrior. You remain a hero in my dreams.

Prologue

This is for the girls who have *yet* to forgive themselves. Girls with skin darker than dark. Girls with too much fat where the ideology of beauty lies. Girls who, because they have stomachs that fold like envelopes and dimples on their thighs that jiggle like dessert on Christmas Day, would never make it in beauty pageants or onto the cover of a magazine.

This... is for the girls who have *yet* to forgive themselves. Girls who have loved other girls with about as much ferocity in their hearts as it would take to start a war. Girls who have heard the words "big" and "thick madam" more times than you hear about skinny bitches on rap songs. Girls who have witnessed too much judgement on the faces of men because they are too much to handle - literally.

This is for the girls who have mastered the art of deception, and the "I'm sorry" because they are too afraid to stand out and be themselves. For girls who have silenced their voices in the hopes of averting even more attention; and for girls who walk around with faces that say: How I wish a scoundrel would say something. Girls who are eloquent in the language of pain, and have cried themselves to sleep more times than it takes you to hit the "like" button.

This is for girls who may fall short but deserve love nonetheless - worthy of finding comfort in the sturdy arms of men with voices that roar. Girls so tall they could hear God sigh in heaven. This is for the girls who have *yet* to forgive themselves.

So, you loved a man with such a roving eye that he could never really appreciate the beauty that is you. You wanted him, and you had him, but then you woke up and found that he had snuck out the night before - with your heart in a disposable bag, ready to throw to the dogs. The selfish bastard! You need to forgive yourself.

So, after you believed when they said that "fat girls cannot be loved", you stuck your finger down your throat and starved yourself till it could not carry the weight of all the men that had left you naked and alone. You beat down your body and named every stretch mark on your thighs, under your belly and in-between the places where light never shines... and you grew angry. You need to forgive yourself.

So, you asked God for a man's heart, but you know that God doesn't work like that. You stole his heart instead, asked God for forgiveness, and then went ahead and broke it. You need to forgive yourself, because this is for you - for girls who have *yet* to forgive themselves.

Tlhalefo

CHAPTER 1

Hair, hair, glory

There's a skill to doing black hair. From the hot combs to the perm, to gently and steadily sowing the weave to not drive the needle into someone's brain, washing hair so well that what was once a proud afro is now a sleek and manageable ponytail, and applying that award-winning relaxer just long enough to do the job and not burn the scalp. Every hairstylist knows that hell hath no fury like a client with a burnt scalp.

The same applies to braiding. From an effortless twist to very heavy box braids, straight backs, and straight ups so tight that they stretch your eyes to half their size - rendering you strikingly beautiful but finding it nearly impossible to sleep for the first few days without cussing the hairdresser because you are unable to turn your head at will.

The skill is that some stylists care enough not to pull your hair back so far it looks as if you had your head resized; while some don't care as much. So negligent that a month later you are walking around with a receding hairline, picking tufts of your hair from the floor every time you have to comb your tresses.

If you don't want to end up looking like Suzy-with-the-bald-patches, the skill is to keep your hair moisturized at all times and come back to have it washed because you were advised that this would keep it healthy and avoid split ends. Personally, I have never understood the excitement of split ends. I believe the term was coined to make hairless women feel better about themselves.

"Hey, Ntombi! I'm here for my appointment." It's very warm this Saturday morning in the Mother City, 22 degrees with a light breeze, and I have an overdue date with my laptop, some ice cream, and a marathon of *Sex and the City.* Oh, Carrie baby!

"Hey, Zee! How have you been, darling?"

"I've been good. I see you went blonde this time." I try to hide the hint of surprise in my voice but fail. She smiles, regardless, her gold tooth glistering.

"Yes, I did. Do you like?"

"Of course! Is it Brazilian?" I ask, and almost lean in to touch it, but remember that I would hate if someone touched my bought hair without my permission. No matter how old you are, or where you are, ask any black girl this and they will tell you: "We hate it when people just come and start digging their nails into our heads". You have no right, sister!

"Peruvian, darling! You should ask Taylor to stop using Brazilian, they are so yesterday." She is almost purring, and I realize she is bragging.

"I will. Is he free?" I look around at the long line of impatient clientele.

"He went out but will be back in twenty minutes. You can sit over there."

"Thanks," I reply and sit down to amuse myself with a bunch of tabloid magazines. There is an old copy with a woman on the cover who looks familiar. Then it hits me... It's Moon's mother. The woman really is gorgeous.

"Do you want something to drink, darling?" Ntombi asks as she does with every customer. I nod, "Water if you have please."

And that is how my conversations go on my visits to Taylor's Hair Dynasty. Ntombi is the incredibly attractive receptionist who sometimes does nails when they are understaffed. She always has her hair styled to the nines and I have immensely envied her many times. With her caramel skin, she can get away with having blonde hair, red hair, and even once went blue. I am unfortunately not that lucky, being a chocolate-skinned girl and all.

I have been a loyal customer of Taylor's ever since coming to Cape Town, to the point that everyone knows my name and the only person who is allowed to touch my hair is Taylor himself. I come here every two months, at least. Once to change the weave, and a second time to wash and style it so I don't look like I have an over-worn, dirty, and smelly mop on my head - and I can tell you that it doesn't come cheap.

Taylor has been doing hair for almost ten years now. His client base includes celebrities, socialites, professionals, and wealthy housewives who have more money than they have obligations. A bundle of Brazilian hair comes at the juvenile price of R600 for 8 inches. And that's just one bundle. A 12-inch bundle costs R900... the more inches you get, the higher the price. A lace wig with a front starts at a staggering R750 for a bob and can go up to R2500 for twenty-two inches. The real jaw-droppers are the Peruvian weaves. A single bundle doesn't cost less than R1000.

I once spent R4500 on three 14-inch bundles, including labor (all this at a discounted student price from Taylor). Sometimes the price of a weave is determined by style, regardless of length. Whether it is a curly or straight weave... be it black, two-toned, blonde, or even blue. Despite the exorbitant prices, there are extremely loyal women (like me) who have a monthly budget for hair. And if you thought there were limits, people may soon be moving on to Cambodian and Malaysian hair… and God knows how expensive those will be.

I love my weaves. I'm obsessed with a good-looking weave, in fact. And believe me, I've had them all… from massive curls to straight cuts, French braids, the ones with fringes, and lace fronts too. I've gone black, brown, two-toned, and once had dark purple highlights that were only really visible when I stood in the sun. For me, it's not about hating my own hair (as Moon insists), but rather the fact that it takes too much effort to maintain the hair myself. Also, a good weave is instant beauty.

"When was the last time you felt your own hair?" Moon would ask accusingly, anger building in her eyes and her forehead folding, as her dreads banged from side to side.

"I don't know," I would strike back, irritation rising in my own voice. "Why does it even matter?" While I envy her gorgeous locks, I did not have the patience.

"Because you are spending a ridiculous amount of money on hair that is not even yours," she would say; and each time this happens I pray for the floor to open and swallow her whole. God forgive me.

"It is my hair, I bought it!" This was all that mattered.

"Zee, be serious. I have seen your hair and it is gorgeous, but you are too busy hiding it behind the horse tails and dead people's hair." If there is one person who is well-versed in insulting people, that's Moon.

"It's not dead people's hair! I'm contributing to the economy of Vietnam and Brazil. That should count for something."

"You don't even know if the person whose hair you are parading had mad cow disease or an incurable hair infection, and then someone decided to cut their hair off and sell it." Where did she get all of this craziness?

"Please, Moon, now you are the one being ridiculous. The hair gets washed and that is all that matters - other than the fact that it makes me look, and feel, exceptional. And don't you dare throw stones when there are poachers in Braamfontein chopping people's dreads off to sell in the black market. Yours being that long, you should be worried about being a victim and let me deal with my tick-infested Remy weave."

I have been attacked for choosing to hide my hair and embrace weaves more than once, but it's really not about validating my black card or staying true to my roots; it's about wanting to look and feel fabulous and having the platform to do so.

With my natural hair, I could never shower like a white girl or pull a Halle Berry coming out of the pool in that James Bond movie. I would always have to worry about it shrinking... what the chlorine would do to it... having to dry it forever before I could even manage to comb it. But then Mother Nature heard my cries and those of many other black sisters out there and gave us the selfless people of Cambodia, Peru, and Brazil. Today I can straighten "my hair", or curl it when the need arises. My hair!

"Here he comes," Ntombi announces, drawing me out of my daydreams and guiding me to Taylor's chair. Taylor is a stylish, fashion-forward, and beautiful gay man. He is tall, light in complexion, and has a smile so perfectly white it can make anyone envious. He is pleasant, funny, and a hair god - but let no one come between Taylor and his own hair.

I was walking around Long Street the first time I met him, looking for a place where my hair could find delicate hands, and there it was... the Hair Dynasty that managed to turn the sister in me into someone worthy of finding a prince charming. We have done it all... braids, straight updos, weaves (mostly the weaves), and it's as if every time he touches my hair he leaves a little bit of magic.

"You have gorgeous hair, darling," he cooed as soon as I took my beanie off to let him have his way for the first time. "I doubt you ever have to worry about a receding hairline." I laughed. He has a way of making anyone feel welcome.

"I get that a lot, but I do not like showing my hair."

"In God's name, why not? If I had your hair I would not spend a single cent on weaves ever again. But since I don't, and this is a business relationship, I encourage you to spend as much money as you want on me, darling. What can I do for you?" he exclaimed proudly, and we laughed in unison.

"I want to wash it first then put on a weave. Like a Brazilian, but a short one."

"How about a bop? It would suit your face. You have beautiful features, darling."

"I have never done that before but if you promise that I will look good, then yes."

"Darling, I have been doing this for years, trust me! I have turned ugly ducklings into princesses with my magical hands. I will make you look like a million dollars!" He exclaimed as he twirled me in the rolling chair.

"Now you are talking," I say and smile reluctantly because I am weary of giving in so easily; but I am trusting that he is going to do miracles. Heaven knows I hate surprises.

Taylor and I have been inseparable since that warm day in September. I had had people do my hair before but there was something about the way Taylor touched my head that made me comfortable. He took care and was alert in his craft. He noticed that I had cut my hair twice before and that the last person to cut my split ends had done a very bad job at it. It was as if the second he touched your head, he could tell exactly what had happened before. How could I not trust this person?

I learned that day that most things in life have a skill to them and so does doing someone else's hair, and Taylor, with his extravagant hairstyles, long fingers, and sky-scrapper stilettoes was the most skilled person I had ever met.

"Okay, I am done, princess. DONE!" Taylor exclaimed after what seemed like forever - a welcome proclamation as my butt had begun to complain. This was the other thing about Taylor, he did not just do your hair because he could, he took his time and made sure that it was as close to perfection as possible. I twirled in the chair and lifted my head for the first time since he had put his magic hands on me.

I was excited, and nervous because this was the first time I would be rocking a short bob in public. It had to look good... but more importantly, I had to feel good. "I am so nervous," I exclaimed as he went on to bring me another mirror.

"Why should you be? Darling, you have gorgeous features. Believe me, you are doing more justice to this hairstyle than Kim Khumalo."

"Thee Kim Khumalo?" I asked incredulously and laughed. For those of you who don't know, Kim Khumalo is the Beyoncé of South Africa. She is gorgeous, and immensely talented vocally. When she sings, you'd swear an angel was upon us. Every boy lusted after Kim because of her curves and thick lips, and every girl prayed to wake up with non-artificial eyebrows and pimple-free skin like she has. To be compared... no wait... to have Taylor say I looked better than her, even on this one occasion made my ninja-self applaud.

"Yes. I am her personal stylist. Don't tell her this, but she has a really huge forehead." Taylor added with his usual flair and then stood behind me with the mirror. I had to admit, I looked good, maybe not as good as what Kim Khumalo looks when she wakes up, but I felt good, and that was a skill that I learned Taylor possessed. The skill is not only to do good hair but to even make one feel better about themselves. "You like?"

"Are you kidding me? I love," I said, holding back a scream.

"Well, once again I have surprised myself." Taylor bragged and we both laughed.

"I really love," I whispered more to myself this time. Taylor did not hear me. I was so excited I was already planning to take a picture of my new hairdo and send it to my mother and sister. There are a lot of things the women in my family have in common, and one of them is the love of good hair. In her prime, my mother still spends about the same amount of money, time, and effort on her hair as she had when she was in her twenties.

My sister co-owns a salon with a high school friend of hers and can tell you what hairstyle was the in fashion, how much it cost, and how long it would last before it even hit the commercial streets. No one can come between her and her crown. "Sis, I don’t trust a woman with a bad hairstyle. It’s like a man wearing white shoes, or flip-flops with socks. There is something devious about a woman who does not put effort into flaunting a good hairstyle,” she would say, as I sat and admired her tresses.

Growing up, our mother made sure that my sister and I always had our hair in check from as early as the time we were in preschool. We were not even allowed to play with sand like most of the neighborhood children who played house. We knew that our mother would either cut our hair off or chase us with a shoe if we even as much as put a grain of sand on our heads.

For a while, the obsession with good hair left me paralyzed with fear but it was only when I was eight when I realized why my mother went beyond to make sure our hair was always healthy. I was coming from the kitchen with a tray larger than my short hands could carry, spilling the cup of coffee she had asked me to make, when I saw it. For the best part of my childhood, I had always believed that my mother’s hair was hers because she took such great care; but around the time when I was starting preschool, my mother became sick and had to be hospitalized for a long while.

I remember crying so much because I could not understand what was happening to our family, but I actually cried because no one could do my hair the way she could. My sister, only five years older than me, tried to step in and take over the job, but it was just not the same. Although she had a skill in handling my hair and knew when to use which comb, something was missing… My mother's touch.

So, as I stood there hidden behind the doorway with the now half cup of coffee and biscuits, I saw something that made even the hair, on my own head stand on end. My mother had taken off her wig (something I had no clue she even owned), and she did not have any hair on her now shiny bald head. The sight hurt me more than it was supposed to. Apart from feeling sorry for her, I had never in a million years believed my mother, (with the kind heart and warm smile, whom I trusted more than the sugar in my coffee) had deceived me into believing she had real hair. How did she manage to take such diligent care of her daughters' hair when she didn't have any?

My mother must have felt my presence at the doorway because she turned and gave me one of her warm smiles. "Oh don't worry, baby, it will grow back again. It's just cancer." She said it with such little effort, like it was not even a big deal, as if this was something our family was accustomed to seeing. Like my eight-year-old self did not in any way feel cheated by Mother Nature and the cancer that had stolen my mother's crown... her beautiful hair. "It will grow back again," she said again, with more emphasis in her words, as if to make sure that they did not betray what she actually felt. Life went on uninterrupted as if the big revelation was just another episode in the Zungu household.

For years after I was obsessed with good hair, or at the very least the idea of it. I took care of my edges, kept my hair moisturized and healthy, and washed once a month, minimum. The fear of becoming like my mother was what forced me to hide my own hair. I lived my life cushioned by the comfort that extensions and weaves provided. Afraid that if I tried to connect with my hair I might become too attached, and then it would hurt much when the cancer came for me too, and the chemotherapy took it all away.

"Zimkhita," my sister whispered as soon as I came home from a netball match that we had lost, drenched in sweat and sheltering blisters that cried through the soles of my feet.

"Can I at least be allowed to take a few breaths and drink a glass of water before you remind me that it is my turn to do the chores? I swear, Nam-Nam, I just want the earth to open up and swallow me whole. Every part of my body hurts," I complained, as my body relentlessly hit the kitchen floor, unassisted. I was *kaput.*

"Zimkhita?" she whispered again and this time I paid attention. The low tone in her voice said that she was trying hard not to be heard.

"What is it?" I asked as I forced my eyelids to remain open. No amount of netball losses and overworked thunder-thighs could make me overlook the fact that my sister was calling out my name as if her next breath depended on it.

"Mama is sick again..."

"What?"

"The cancer is back again." She replied and immediately looked behind her back, her huge eyes rolling upwards. It was as if she had just heard someone, or rather something, break. I didn't know it then, but I later realized that something did break that day... my heart. I didn't cry, scream, shout, or throw things like the people usually do on reality television when they hear bad news.

In our family, cancer was like the uninvited uncle who got drunk at parties, kissed you with stinky breath, and told everyone how proud of you he was. He would embarrass you, and you had no retribution because he would start cussing and throwing things around the moment he was upset. He may even hurt you if you were not careful. So, you had to smile and pretend to laugh at his not-so-funny stories and endure the breath that struck your nostrils like a slap on the face. You had to tolerate him until he either fell asleep or grew tired of you. The cancer that our mother had was that uncle who merely came to make his presence known and everyone feel uncomfortable, because... well, he didn't care.

The one thing I was worried about, apart from my mother making a full recovery (as she usually did), was how she would feel about having to lose all of her hair again. It may have been stupid and selfish but every night when I prayed, I asked God to save her hair.

CHAPTER 2

Therapy for black girls

"I hope you never fall in love, Moon, because you will never be the same." He said this right after I told him I wanted to see other people, and that our arrangement was not working for me. "You spend so much time running that you don't know when to just sit back and play defense. I hope you never know what a broken heart feels like."

I stood there, confused. I could not understand why my childhood friend, who was the first person I had been intimate with, was being such a wuss about having his feelings hurt. He should have been happy. I was letting him go so he could live his life and play as many girls as he could, break as many hearts as he wills... yet, here he was telling me I was the bad "guy".

"Motswedi, you're being dramatic, I told you this was not a relationship," I replied, flicking my dreadlocks to the side.

"And that is the problem with you Moon, you don't know how to act like a girl."

"Please, just because I don't conform to society's ideals of how a girl should act doesn't mean I don't have female genitalia. There is nothing wrong with being sexually curious and wanting to explore what desire and who I'm attracted to. The problem is that you disagree."

"That's because girls cannot be as sexually explorative as guys," he retorted with arrogance, very much convinced by his ignorance. I almost gagged.

"Says who? We have desires too and we can get sex, can't we?'

"That's not the point, and you know it. When guys sleep around it is power play but when girls sleep around it's seen as being loose. Look at it this way... a guy is like a house. Its value increases with every buyer. A girl, on the other hand, is like a car whose value depreciates with the mileage. The second a woman loses her innocence, her value in society decreases."

"You sound so redundant I almost believed it. Anthropologically speaking, women are more hormonal and more curious than men. It's science, Mo."

"But science and anthropology do not get you laid, do they?"

"And neither does a twisted view of what we should do with our bodies. I mean, which gender generally controls the sex?"

"The guys. We put it down," he said, and I laughed, very loudly.

"No you don't, we choose whether we want to sleep with you when we want to do it, and for how long. Our arrangement was a perfect example of that."

"Moon you're just a control freak. You don't even count."

"No, I'm a girl who's aware of her body and how it works. If and when I want to get laid, I should be allowed to do so without inciting people to write my name on cardboards and go picketing. I mean, you have slept with at least three girls during the time that we have been together."

"And that's because I am a guy. I am at the beginning of my sexual prime."

"Biologically, yes; but that does not excuse the fact that you're being insensitive to the girls who naively believe that they are the only ones you are getting it on with. You have a choice not to engage with that many girls, but you choose to, regardless." Honestly, how could he not even see this?

"I am sorry if this rubs your feministic views the wrong way, but I am a guy. I am wired in a way that makes me unable to resist sex or physical attraction."

"That is not an excuse. You have ten fingers and I have ten fingers. You have a brain, and you have eyes, and you can talk and walk and think and run fast when your adrenalin pumps... the same things I can do. Why does sex have to be different?"

"I have balls and you don't."

"Yes, but biologically those are just sexual organs and I have my own, don't I?"

And it was in that moment when Motswedi could not justify why society treated me differently from him when it came to sex, that I made a vow to never be sucked into the marginalized ideologies of how people were bound to perceive me if I dared think any different to them.

We had grown up playing hide and seek from the time we were snotty five-year-olds at preschool, and later succumbed to the addictions to video games. I had been reading a book and he was playing cars with the other boys the first day we met. He walked over and told me that he wanted to read the book I had in hand. He acted entitled like that. I said no and he called me a stupid girl. I punched him in the nose and he bled.

The teacher told me to go to the naughty corner, and my parents were called. My mother, with her designer handbag and fiery red lipstick (her trademark since the early days of her modeling career), was mortified and promised the teacher that anything like that would never happen again. I didn't care... because it was my father who's approval I sook. He, with his mustache and a raspy voice that made him growl when he spoke. He had taught me that I should defend myself against everyone, and I assumed that included snotty, entitled five-year-old boys. I was right.

"For goodness sake, Mathapelo! The boy started it."

"Baks, how could you even say that?" my mom asked, her nose flaring.

"Because I was a five-year-old boy once," my father replied, and I smiled victoriously.

"But she is a girl, she should have told him off instead of breaking his nose. I, like you, want her to grow up to be independent and powerful, but to use her words not her fists," my mother scolded and stormed out, the sound of her high heels clicking in the hallway.

I got a long lecture from my mother that night, about how being a strong woman meant more than throwing my fists around. "Everywhere you go men run the world, and regardless of how unfair that is, it is the reality. I do not want you to ever quieten yourself because anyone feels like you are too much for them, or because you are trying to fit in. I want you to roar every time you say something, Moon, but I don't want you to look like a reality TV girl while at it." Of course, I wanted to listen to my mother. She was always so regal-looking and poised and commanded respect everywhere she went. People liked her a lot.

"But he started it, mommy. He wanted the book that I was reading. I couldn't hand it to him. I was reading." Despite my defense, my mother still believed that I should not have punched Motswedi in the nose as a way of letting him know that I was reading the book. "It's called being a lady," she said.

My father, however, did not share the sentiment. He was proud that I had stood up for myself, even though he dared not show this to my mother. "How did you punch him?" he asked when it was just the two of us.

"Just the way you showed me. Under the nose," I replied proudly, swinging my fist in the air.

"Oooh, that's my girl!" He exclaimed, and my heart somersaulted in pride. I was very close to my father. I admired everything about him. He was always telling me stories or teaching me some new trick, and that fascinated my five-year-old mind.

Years later I became very good friends with this same boy, and when our bodies began acknowledging the long list of unanswered questions, and desires, drawn up by the biology at work, it was logical that he would be the one I turned to for my first sexual encounter. Motswedi is arrogant and entitled, sometimes a little self-absorbed - but he was shaken when I first made the proposal.

"I like you, Moon, as a friend, because you're not like other girls. To me, you're almost like a guy, but this is different, I cannot take your virginity."

"I didn't ask you to take anything, Mo. We are just having sex," I said, making sure to not get any wires crossed.

"Is that what you think it will be? I don't want to be the guy you end up hating for the rest of your life."

"If I hate you it will be because you're insulting my intelligence. Why should it be a big deal that you are the first guy I have sex with? You act like you were born with a degree in the subject, or did you somehow get stuck on the girl you first had sex with?"

"Hey, we are not talking about me okay? I have graduated from that night."'

"If I remember correctly, you were not so pompous afterward," I retorted, knowing very well that I would strike a chord. Motswedi was an egomaniac, so any reference to his manhood would certainly cripple him. He was at the age where boys grew beards, and his face was still as soft as a baby's bum… that had to sting.

"Look, don't bring that experience up, okay!? I was young and inexperienced. I have grown from that. Very much, if I have to say it myself." That part he was right about.

"We all have to start somewhere, Mo. Let's not make this out to be something it's not."

In the end, I managed to convince him that it was just sex, that our friendship would not be compromised in any way, and that I had chosen him not because I was into him but because he always bragged about how his third leg could do things that were not yet legal.

It lasted six months, and regardless of how it ended, I kept my promise, and our friendship survived. You see, I had learned from an early age that love was just an illusion bought into by insecure people who were too busy trying to achieve something they knew nothing about; that what everyone actually wanted was to have someone around when they physically wanted them.

There is nothing wrong with regarding women as sexual beings; in fact, the only thing I have a problem with is when men only see women as that. Mo and I have been good friends for most of my life, and even after our little escapade we still managed to be cordial.

We were sitting in my room another day, talking about the dynamics of boy-girl relationships and sports cars, when he stopped in the middle of the conversation, his eyes lighting up like he had just figured out the cure for cancer: "I get it now. I get why you're this hard person. You're trying to be like your father. You're trying to make him proud aren't you?"

His eyes were twinkling at this realization. He looked proud of himself. I wanted to break his five-second tryst of fame and tell him, I knew he would see right through me. Could it be true? I didn't even know how that could explain anything. "Look, you're a cool chick, I love that about you. But you go around burning your bridges as soon as you get over them, and hell that may be okay because you're like super rich, but everyone needs someone."

I could see where this was going, and I was not having it. I hated it when people tried to figure me out and came up with all these explanations about why I did what I did. Honestly, it was not like I came from a broken home or that I hadn't felt loved. I came from a perfect home and my parents (in their separate ways) had showered me with enough love to prevent me from self-destruction.

"I have seen what you do when people try to get close to you," he added, sombrely.

"What do I do, Dr. Phil? Or should I call you Iyanla-fix-my-life?"

"You're doing it again," he said and winked conspiratorially.

"Doing what, clown? I am asking you a question."

"No, you're diverting."

"Diverting? Motswedi please, even I know that's not part of your everyday grammar, out here trying to be a psychologist."

"Don't judge me okay, I watch Oprah with my girlfriend."

I laughed. "Which one? Please tell me it's Neo. I like that one."

"I have one girlfriend, okay! Damn! You did it again and you're so good you don't even realize it. Look, I might not know what it feels like to grow up with people wanting to know what happens in your life or judging everything you do or post on social media, but I know you. You're a nice person when you're not playing defense, and you have to let people know that about you. Do you know why no guy has asked you out or why the other girls hate you?"

"No, and I couldn't give a rat's ass," I answered without flinching, and I meant it.

"The guys feel intimidated by you and the girls say you act like you're better than everyone," Motswedi continued, ignoring my statement.

"But I am!"

"You're doing it again, Moon. You have to stop."

The truth was that Motswedi was completely right. Although I could never admit it to his face, I wanted to be like my father, if not better. No matter how hard it was to admit, I knew that I never wanted to disappoint him in any way. I was going to be the model daughter, and nothing was going to stand in my way.

My father regarded me as a son more than a daughter. To him, I was the boy he never had and although he would never say it out loud, I was smart enough to know that he wished I was a boy. He spoke to me about relationships with women and how to go about with them and never once did I hear him mention the idea of me with a boy.

My mother loathed this, and she did not hide any of her feelings on the subject matter. "Bakang, you have to stop treating Moon like a boy. She is a girl. She is allowed to kiss a few frogs before getting to her prince charming. You need to stop treating your daughter like it's a crime to be a girl."

But my mother's words must have flown right over our heads because my father and I continued talking about open palm slaps and nothing much about who would have to deal with the collateral damage, as if we knew that I would be causing it soon enough.

While my mother tried her very best to raise me as a lady, my father did quite the opposite - raising me to be a fighter. My young self could not fathom why there had to be a difference. Why being a lady could not go hand in hand with being a fighter. How could raising a fist be a determiner of whether you were regarded as feminine or not?

"I'm sorry Mr. and Mrs. Mosiapoa but we have no choice except to suspend Moon for a week." This was Mrs. Grubber, my primary school headmistress with her bangs and round-rimmed spectacles. Her sharp pointed nose looked thinner than usual, but it was her forehead that caught my attention.

"How bad was it?" my mother asked, making sure to avoid locking eyes with me. She was always photo-ready, dressed in her knee-high boots, and fiery red Rimmel lipstick, and spoke eloquent English; and as expected, she was asking all the right questions.

"She broke the other girl's nose causing massive blood clots that needed stitches." Mrs. Grubber answered softly and dramatically, as if she was delivering a eulogy. I noticed, with sudden interest, that Mrs Grubber had an awful way of delivering bad news. My mother turned in her seat and this time, looked me right in the eye.

"Moon, how could you? You could have killed the other child."

I know that I answered in my head because I knew better than to have my mother hear me say, "I know, but I had to punch her, Ma. I had to do it for you". I lowered my eyes, refusing to look into my mother's eyes and see the disappointment.

"She started it," I mumbled after suffering in silence for too long. But no one, not even my supposed-to-be-proud father said a word, and at that moment I felt a deep sense of loneliness that I had never felt before. It scared me.

CHAPTER 3

I should be black, but I am white

Some white girl at school had said that I was "impure", and I remember my mother - a loud, vibrant, and spirited Xhosa woman with a very visible behind and a thick voice that ricocheted across the room when she talked - telling me, as I sat on the bathroom floor bawling my eyes out, "You have got to put those tears right back where they come from, child. Because I am not having any of it."

As a "colored" child I may have not belonged with either of the two major races, but to call me impure must have been the lowest form of prejudice and ignorance in a country is supposed to be democratic.

Yes, my mother is very much the black woman who listens to Brenda Fassie and wears a doek on her head when she goes to bed, and my father is a white man who spends most of his time trying hard not to insult his daughter. This means that my skin is too light, my ass is too big and my hair is neither long, silky, nor is it the right type of natural hair that people brag about - it's just soft.

I've had people snicker behind my back because my skin is not black enough. I've had people (black people for that matter) call me names because I have "nice" hair, and I've had white people look at me sideways because I have my father's green eyes. A "black" girl with nappy hair and green eyes... they must find this so bizarre.

When you are five years old and still trying to learn the rules of chess on how to get what you want from either parent, and still sleep with your imaginary friend (thumb thrust deep in your mouth), it is hard to figure out why someone like Hannah Woodsen would call you impure in a class full of other snotty five-year-olds... but she did and Lord knows I may have been too young to appreciate the gravitas of her insult but I felt the word pierce my heart after it flew from her mouth.

That day I went home as someone who had no idea where they belonged, not as Melissa McFarland. Was I black, like my mother who has chocolate skin and dimples that made her the most beautiful woman I have ever seen; or was I white like my father with wavy brown hair that clung to his forehead when he perspired and skin that turned pink whenever he stayed in the sun too long? Or was Hannah Woodsen right...Was I impure?

My parents broke up when I was five, and my mom married among her people the second time around. My father did the same, and even though they are both happy in their new and improved lives, it does feel awkward having siblings who are not a mixed race and being the only one caught between two worlds. I won't lie, I sometimes feel resentment bubbling when I am with members on either side of my family and people dare say that I am too black to belong to my white side of the family or that I am too white to belong to the other side.

I end up having to explain the fact that it was not my fault that my father was a rich and spoiled kid who wanted to piss his prim and proper parents off by marrying a black girl from the village. That my mom was naive enough to believe that she could fall in love with a white boy of a race that had oppressed her people for centuries, and whose mom called her "a nobody" to her face.

There are instances where my eyes turn a darker shade of green and my nose red. I've asked my mom why I wasn't downright black or "pure" white... Why I had to be the odd one out. Why Claire and Luke had it easy, and why wouldn't Mxolisi and Sibahle never had to endure being called names?

It must have pained her because for the first time she held me tightly at the shoulders, like I was about to do something illegal, and said... "I always knew at one point that my choices would haunt you, but I always thought your dad would be around to help me deal with it all. I can't change how you look, I wouldn't want to, but I want you to know that you have to love yourself because no one can do for you." It wasn't what I had expected her to say, but it was enough to comfort me.

"I did not plan on falling in love with a white boy, let alone have a child with him, and maybe it was gullible for me to expect people to be accepting but you have got to understand that people only judge you because they either do not understand or are not ready for change. Also, you will not get anywhere if you keep looking back to check who your cheerleaders are. Your father and I may have not been ready for interracial marriage, but we did love each other, and we love you more than anything."

My mother's courage gave context to this saying by Azra Tabassum. Although I discovered their author much later, they have given meaning to the better part of my life:

"I will teach my daughter not to wear her skin like a drunken apology. I will tell her, make a home out of your body, live in yourself, do not let people turn you into a regret, do not justify yourself. If you're a disaster you're the most beautiful one I've ever seen. Do not deconstruct from the inside out, you belong here, you belong there, not because you're lovely but because you're more than that."

It was because of them that I decided that crying would be the last thing I do whenever some silly white boy asked if my eyes were contacts because I looked weird as a black girl with green eyes. I knew better than to cower when he continued, with the worst attitude one could muster, that he would date me only if I didn't look so black.

I knew not to whimper if some black girl called me a white snob because merely liking her boyfriend's picture on social media apparently meant that I was flirting with him. To laugh it off when they said, "There is too much of you and very few of us. Who is supposed to love us if you keep taking all of our men?" I also knew to wear my skin thick and to accept that I would always be "too black" for my white people and "too white" for my black people. My name is Melissa McFarland, and this is my story.

I'm with my mother in town, and she has been dragging me from shop to shop comparing prices, trying to figure out why Checkers sugar costs more than Pick n Pay's. I follow in silence, although my feet hurt like crazy. None of my siblings ever go anywhere with our mother, but I am always caught with a spineless refusal strangled halfway down my throat because I am the obedient one, unfortunately so.

"Look at this, Melly. These people are getting their prices from heaven. How do they sell 2kg of sugar for R24.99? I swear they think that we grow money on trees. Tyhini!" she proclaims, surprised, and I just nod my head and pretend to be bothered by the ridiculousness of these prices. I'm not though, but you can't pay me enough to tell that to my mother.

She, however, does not stop here but calls one of the assistants, "excuse me, Sisi, why are your prices so high? Are you trying to rob the poor?" But the lady is either as shocked as I am or doing a great job at pretending to be. She looks past my mom and, unaware that we're together, whispers enough venom to steer my judgment, "You know black people and their broke tendencies."

I'd like to preserve my innocence, so I don't say anything. I just closed my eyes and let the insult slide. I've heard much worse in my many years of living - I'm just glad my mother missed this one, or else she would have brought the whole shop down. You should know better than to mess with a black woman doing grocery shopping with a calculator in hand. Just don't do it!

"You would think that in this new South Africa they would at least be willing to dig deeper into their pockets and stop being so stingy. You know, with them taking all the money for themselves?" I don't, but still say nothing. My mother, ignorant of this exchange, is busy trying to figure out why the low-fat costs more than the full cream.

"Melly mtanam, these people are giving me a headache with their prices. We will go check eSpar. But your sister said she wants the low fat, neh?" I don't answer. When my mother asks a question, I've learned, she doesn't really want an answer. She just wants to hear the sound of her voice. I think this is just a thing all parents do.

"Look at her. I swear this is why I stopped being a waitress. They never tip you and if they do, it's not even 10 percent of how much they spend." This lady clearly has a lot to say. "Be glad she is not your mother." But I've had enough.

"She is my mother!" I scream so loud that my mother drops the can of baked beans she was holding, and the look on the coloured assistant's face is priceless. The white girl in me shouted louder than I had planned to, and I know I must look crazy. The sad truth was that this was not my first experience of this kind, and I was confident that it would not be the last.

When we were out in public people gave more respect to me than they did to my mother, and we once had a shop assistant at a fancy boutique search my sister Sibahle's handbag, but not mine. My family is blind to this sort of thing. They aren't bothered by it as much as I am, but as someone who's trying to find her place in the world, it causes me a great deal of distress.

When I am out with my dad and his family it seems as though things happen faster than they do with the other family, and with more respect. The waitresses are extra polite and more efficient. They tend to be more courteous, our food does not take longer than twenty minutes to arrive after the order has been placed. Once, Sibahle and I had to wait for two hours before the food reached our table, and it was not even that sophisticated a meal. Just burgers and chips. And before you say it's because my mother spends a lot of time comparing prices... it's also a thing my stepmother does. It's not about color when it comes to grocery shopping, it's just that most women are bent on being frugal.

"What's wrong with you?" my mother asks, completely bewildered by my outburst. "You need to control yourself when you're in public, my child."

I nod in agreement and hope she lets this one go. Heaven knows that I'd witness another World War if she finds out what the shop assistant has been saying behind her back.

"Mama, can I go wait for you in the car, my feet hurt from all this walking."

"And who is going to push the trolley, Melisa? Me? You would think that having children meant that they got to do things for you, but Thixo I have the laziest children on earth! I'd swear you do this on purpose." I sigh and push the trolley, happy to have my mother back.

Hannah Woodsen is like the reincarnation of the evil stepsister you wish you never meet, and this is why we were never friends. She had the bluest of eyes, and beautiful, blonde pigtail locks that she could fling to one side at whim and reached down her back. The first time I saw her I remember thinking that she may have been a magical creature, but she had very thin lips, hardly smiled, and could cry on cue whenever she wanted something.

She had hosted sleepovers by the time we got to the third grade - lots of them - and I was never invited to any. I was not okay at first, I was only five years old and was allowed to feel otherwise of way about not getting an invite to a sleepover. You can call it insecurity, but we saw it as a rite of passage.

While she was able to rock bangs one day and pigtails the next, I had to wait for those Sunday afternoons when my mother back came from church and we sat outside, me on her lap, while she drove a cold, metallic afro comb into my hair and braided it to last the week, so she wouldn't be forced to see to with my "unmanageable" hair on the daily.

It was never okay on Sundays. I looked forward to those afternoons sessions because they always ended with me in tears, causing my mother to stop, look into my eyes, and give me an ultimatum:

"You have two choices, Melissa. Either I cut your hair and you look like the boys in your class, or I braid your hair and you look like a decent girl."

Of course, this had me biting my tongue and stifling the tears., and my mother, unmoved, would continue driving the comb through my hair as if it owed her something. I did not want her to cut my hair, regardless of how much pain I felt. Not only did not want to be looking like the boys in my class, I knew Hannah Woodsen would never overlook me coming to school with a bald head. I may not have had a clear idea of exactly who I was at the time or of the image I was supposed to present to the world, but people like Hannah Woodsen made the very thought of being different unbearable.

"How is it that your mother is black? She probably somehow colored your skin so you could be lighter." She said this once while we were sitting, listening to Miss Faith read us a story.

"Hannah, keep quiet!" Miss Faith scolded, but it was too late. The girl was more evil than all the villains on television.

"One day you are going to fall asleep and wake up black," she snickered. I clammed up, trying to keep myself from crying.

CHAPTER 4

Nobody wants the black girl struggle

"I have never understood the whole debacle with white on black or black on white racism in democratic South Africa, Moon. I mean we have had over 20 years of freedom and there are still people who are bitter over something that happened way before they were even born. I cannot fall into that ignorance. People need to move on. I mean I fell in love with an awesome guy whose color I don't see." Zimkhita argued passionately. Moon just looked at her friend and shook her head in disbelief.

"Zee... Girl can you not be so damn naive? You cannot tell me that you don't see racism wherever you go. They don't have to call you the k-word for it to constitute racism, it's in their attitude." But Zimkhita was having none of it.

"You see my friend that is exactly the type of thinking that makes it hard for us to move on from all that."

"Please, just because you're getting your hump on with a white boy doesn't mean that you're now in their part of the world. You need blonde hair, blue eyes, a trust fund, and come from a line of people who helped orchestrate Apartheid to truly exist or be fully accepted in their circles."

"Moon, your problem is that you're too passionate. You take black consciousness a little too seriously. Remember how in your first year at varsity you always wrote short stories about people who add no substance to your life? Thomas Sankara, Steve Biko, Kwame Nkrumah..."

"Stop right there, Zee! There are things about you that I will never understand, but you won't hear me being disrespectful. I may be too conscious, but at least I am not bleaching my skin, attaching fake boobs, and flaunting fake hair that comes from people and places I don't even know."

"Well... if I want Gabe and me to be compatible..." and it was at that moment that I switched off.

I have been friends with Zimkhita for about two years now. We started as roommates and that is where our friendship grew from. She was bubbly, and opinionated, and draws pictures so weird they'd make for an animated discussion on the essence of art.

We were similar in a lot of ways, but she sang better. Her family was neither poor nor rich. They were working class South Africans, and for a while, I hid the fact that I had grown up in a mansion that came with a chauffeur and staff at my beck and call. That my father was Bakang Mosiapoa the late uMkhonto we Sizwe stalwart, and that my mom, Mathapelo Khama-Mosiapoa - a former beauty queen originally from Botswana - still graced magazine covers as if she had not aged a single bit in the last twenty years.

Both my parents valued education more than what the number of zeros one had in the bank account or what the beauty they possessed could do for them, so they sent me to the best schools, pilled African literature in every corner of the house, and breathed black consciousness into my little lungs from a young age - like it was the very pump I needed for my asthma.

My mom taught me never to be bitter. After all, her home country was still colonized by the British despite what the media was trying to make the outside world believe. She believed that a bitter heart would cloud my judgment and I had to always move beyond the heartache. She said to never apologize for being exactly who I was, even if it meant that other people would be uncomfortable.

She was good-natured and a little reserved if you didn't know her very well (the complete opposite of my father), but if you made a mistake, she was lethal. At night while other kids were being read bedtime stories about *Cinderella* and *Sleeping Beauty*, she would preach to me, "Black skin the color of raisins. Embrace your kinks that knot at the tip of your fingers, your big butt and flat nose, and the fact that you will always be judged for being different; but never embrace racism in any form, color or degree. Fight it, nana, because if racism goes unchallenged it becomes the norm and before we know it we are back to bending over backwards for people who are shades lighter. Never embrace inferiority."

And yes, while my mom made me read up on Patrice Lumumba, W.E.B. Du Bois, Steve Biko, Martin Luther King, and other black revolutionaries, my father would have easily given me a machete and encouraged me to use violence as a form of anarchy. I understood only after his death that to him violence had been a way of life.

My father lived through the worst of Apartheid. He had seen bulldozers tear down people's homes and sometimes run over those who were not fast enough. He lived through massacres that had ended the lives of his people... his family, and his friends. Yet, he had to accept this and move on without compalin. He was tortured because he spoke too much, detained because he organized marches, and starved for days on end. They called him die swart gevaar, and though he experienced all this, he picked himself up like nothing like this had happened, and soldiered on.

He studied Law at Wits University but was forced to leave because the discrimination against black students was at its helm, and that is when he decided that the best revenge would not come from round tables discussions but from fighting the white man's hatred with hatred. It's a miracle he persisted, but he did, and then he met my mom, and I was born. His favorite saying was "You cannot just forgive and forget when there is no apology, the same way you cannot put a plaster on a gash made by a machete and hope it heals."

My father, Bakang Mosiapoa was the smartest man I knew, and also the most damaged. I will forever look at my mother as a very strong woman for being able to love a broken man. Many people believe that my life was made easier because of my father's legacy and my mother's name, but it's nothing like that. I've heard the sounds of a grown man crying in the middle of the night, and I can tell you, matter-of-factlty, that it is nothing to enjoy.

I have seen people without limbs (because they were unfortunate victims of parcel bombs) and I have seen the unaskable pain on a mother's face as she elaborates on how she last saw her son, or husband, or daughter in 1978. Thirty-six years later, all she prays for is to know what happened. She has accepted their death and just wants to know where their remains are so she can give them a decent burial. This woman is old, her body is riddled with pain, yet she is still holding on to the hope of knowing the fate that befell her children before she goes to her own death bed.

People think, because I grew up in an upmarket Pretoria home where with dinner parties that included a previous president of the country and went to one of the most expensive schools in the land, I don't know what poverty is; but I have seen young black girls use socks and t-shirts as sanitary towels because they are too poor to afford any in the new dispensation. I have seen young black boys lost without a sense of direction, trapped by the vices they know too well, gangsterism. I have slept in a mud house in Lohalape where the family has one cow to milk, and they work on farms to make ends meet. I have met young black girls who performed abortions on themselves because they couldn't afford to walk 20 kilometres to the nearest clinic in the deepest parts of Kwa-Zulu Natal.

I get angry when privileged white people treat these injustices like we deserve them. That just because I am black, I can live with them. I get furious when I am called bitter and angry because I make a noise about them. When someone like Zee, who is entirely black herself, plays the 'it's been 20 years" card just because her hedges are being trimmed by a white boy from Europe with a trust fund, who will never have hassles getting a job from his father, uncle, or grandfather's mining company which ironically hires her own people to work under inhumane conditions for a mere 20 cents per hour.

I then understood my father's stance on forgiveness. "Hmph! Talk about the angry black child. South Africa is a sick child with a disease that is slowly gnawing at her patience and tolerance; and until the day black South Africans can wake up to the sound of an apology and not being called monkeys, savages, imbeciles... When the white man will humble himself to the fact that this country is not his (and was never his to take to begin with)... When black workers are no longer dehumanised, being made to eat their faeces and drink their pee... When a black man can walk into a shop and not be labelled a thief... We may talk of peace, reconciliation and the rainbow nation, but there will never be a cure for this sick child until that day arrives. The condition of this country will continue to deteriorate up till her eventual death."

Alzheimer's took away the man I knew as my father. He didn't suffer long - within a year of his diagnosis he was clutching me tightly and taking his last breath. I had always known he was broken inside, but it still shocked me to see him that weak. My father was not a weak man. "Whatever you do, always remember that Biko said that the greatest weapon in the hands of the oppressor is the mind of the oppressed. They can take away the land and resources but never let them take your mind," he said, between coughs.

It is ironic that the very mind he treasured was what betrayed him. Those were my father's last words, and I have carried then with me since that day. It memory isn't vague. He was stronger that day than I had seen him be in a very long while. That was Baks Mosiapoa for you.

"So, are we still on for movies this Saturday?" I asked because, despite Zee's adamant beliefs, we had shared moments of fun and laughter on the beach, been together at 2 am crying over lost lovers, and had pulled each other out of depressive episodes as our exam papers had returned with dismal results, seeing us fail regardless of the time and effort we had put into the studying. But then again, even Oprah wasn't built in one day?

"I can't. I'm going bowling with Gabe. I swear I'll make it up to you." I rolled my eyes.

"Girl please the only thing you swear by is Gabe and his manhood."

"Which is very good, if you were to try it." she teased.

"Eeew! He's your raggedy surfer boyfriend. Besides, he's not my type." I snorted and we both burst out laughing.

CHAPTER 5

Excuse me, Miss

I met Gabe at the library. Studying, I sat waiting for Moon, but she was running late as usual. He walked over lazily, his shoulders broad, and asked if he could borrow my calculator because he had forgotten his. We were in the same practical group for Photography and I was quite familiar with his face, but he had not once talked to me. So, you can imagine my surprise when this tall guy with brown hair, grey eyes, and the cutest smile came over and asked for *my* calculator.

"If you can't, it's okay, I can..." he stumbled.

"What happened to your calculator?" I asked accusingly, without even meaning to.

What was wrong with me? I had secretly crushed on this guy from a distance and it hadn't gone past a few lingering looks and awkward passes.

"Woah! Sorry! I just need a calculator."

His eyes caught my smile. "I got that part. I'm still waiting to hear where yours is." I wanted to punch myself right in the throat for acting like I was an immature teen. This wasn't going the way I wanted it to. Why was I being so difficult? How was I supposed to act anyway?

"Okay, let me rephrase. The calculator was just an excuse. I'd like to get to know you better."

But the look that I gave him made Gabe quickly add, "Okay, I think you're cool. I would like to take you out for lunch or something."

And for obvious reasons, I remained silent for a while before coming in for the kill: "Why? Do I look anorexic or hungry to you?"

"No, no, that's not it..." He was lost for words, and it wasn't a good look. When I later asked what went through his mind at that moment he said that I was proving to be more difficult than Derek had said I'd be.

He was about to leave when I abruptly intercepted, "Where do you usually take the girls on a first date?"

"Uh... Everyone has a choice."

"Well, I am not hungry so we'll go to the beach. You can swim right?"

"Yeah! I surf." And the way he said it made me chuckle in secret.

"Good, you'll teach me!" To which Gabe smiled and walked away thinking, "This girl is something else."

"You're forgetting something," I called out, trying not to be too loud.

"It's too soon for a first kiss don't you think? I haven't even tried to make an impression on you yet." She couldn't help but smile, he noticed. Her eyes twinkled as she did and a dimple made an appearance on the side of her face. She was gorgeous.

"No, you forgot to ask for my name and take the calculator." He was witty and more relaxed than other boys his age, it was refreshing. I concealed a smile and threw a high-five to my inner diva.

"Oh, I know your name, but if you want mine it's Gabriel Keogh. Gabe for short, and the calculator was really just an excuse."

He was still impressing me on a daily a year later. We had spent days concealed under sheets, our bodies intertwined, hiding from the world because we enjoyed the intimacy we shared. We'd both shed tears while watching romantic comedies, and Titanic was one of them. Gabe can't deny that he cried while watching Titanic.

I'm not a fan of water, but I more than once let myself be manipulated to take a dip in the sea (weave, eyelashes, and all), and sometimes surf. I was scared at first, but once I allowed the water to lead me it was the most exhilarating feeling.

Gabe actually loved my umphoqoko - that's pap and amasi to the western world. He'd hum along to The Soil even though he had no idea what they were singing about. Once Moon and I had even dragged him along to one of their concerts, and you don't want to know how that one ended. You could've cut the tension with a knife, literally.

"Your friend hates me, doesn't she?" Gabe asked later that night as we lay in bed, my 16-inch Peruvian weave carelessly strewn all over his face. I laughed but avoided lifting my head and catching a glimpse of his super charming features. His smile was my kryptonite.

"Is that a rhetorical question?"

"You know what I mean," Gabe replied, tickling me. I squealed with laughter, although I don't like being tickled.

"Okay, okay, hate is a bit extreme, but she has her views about interracial relationships."

"Like?"

"What's with the 21 questions? You're not chickening out after all this time, are you?" I was not willing to go down the race route, got enough flak from Moon about it every day. Honestly, sometimes I just wanted people to look beyond color and accept people as they are. I loved Gabe, not because he's a total hunk who's goofy and smart (also loaded), but because he looked at me like I was magic. I often wake up to find him staring, and he managed to make me feel genuinely happy. It didn't happen a lot these days, but I was sure of the feeling.

"I just want to know why. I mean we've been together for over a year, and she has never even said hello to me. She avoids me and pretends as though she has to go somewhere every time she sees me, and this worries me because she is your best friend."

"Not my best, but my closest friend. Moon would choose family over friendship any day even though it's just her and her mom. She is different from us babe. She believes a white man can only be with a black woman because of lust and wants to fulfill some perverted fantasy. Moon is consciously black to the very core. Her reasoning capacity intimidates people. She might not always be right, but she stands by her beliefs, and we clash often - especially when she accuses me of getting fake boobs and whitening my skin."

"Well, have you?" Gabe asked teasingly, and I throw a pillow at him in protest.

"Derek asked why we don't have a YouTube channel."

"About what?" I ask and laugh. With all his cuteness and muscles, Derek is one of those idiotic guys you meet and wonder if they were dropped on their heads as babies.

"About our relationship."'

"Why are we trying to get famous for being in a relationship?" It's hard enough trying to get people close to us to understand that we love each other without having to build a platform for the whole world to add their two cents. "Do you want to be on YouTube?" I ask, narrowing my gaze at Gabe. He is smart enough to suss out my position, yet proceeds to answer, seemingly trying to avoid getting on my wrong side.

"No! I mean... people do it... maybe?"

"Gabriel Keogh, don't you give me that maybe stuff. Is this because we are interracial? Do we have to validate our relationship with the world?" I cannot believe what I'm hearing.

"No, that's not what I meant."

"By all means, tell me what you meant because it sounds to me like you are trying to get famous off of dating a black girl."

"Please, Zee it's not even like that."

I love my boyfriend (make no mistake), but I am not going to be one of those people who will start a YouTube channel and talk about how people still feel uncomfortable about interracial relationships in the 21st century. It's enough that I have to deal with girls giving me dirty looks and guys calling Gabe names in vernec where he cannot understand, and that I have Moon constantly preaching black consciousness. I am not going to give them another reason to let me know who I should and shouldn't fall in love with.

"I don't want you to do anything you are not comfortable with."

"It's not about whether I'm comfortable or not Gabe, I just don't see why I should be corny. I am not going to do things just because you are white. To me, you are just a guy I happened to love. The second I start with the whole labeling shebang then I'm consenting to the very things people are doing to us. If I wouldn't do it with a black guy, why should I do it with you?"

"Okay babe, I get it. I didn't think you would want to, anyway."

"Do you want to?" I ask, my heart refusing to believe that I could just be another black girl Gabe wants to be seen with.

"No. I mean I have done it before, but I know you wouldn't want to."

"There are levels to being in an interracial relationship," I tell myself, as I turn my back to Gabe my back and hide my anger. We're at a point in the relationship where we have to start saying things to each other without fear of being offensive. I don't much like it here.

On our first date, Gabe took me surfing, as he had promised, and it was nothing like I had ever experienced before. I knew how to swim. No problems there. The issue was being half-naked in front of the guy I had secretly liked. And this was not because I had issues with my body in a bikini (gosh! I could rock a skimpy bikini better than a runway model), the trouble was the hair. This was the does-not-come-cheap yet a very-much-worth-it type of hair that I fawned over.

We swam. We splashed about. He chased me as I tried to run away from the waves, and even attempted to teach me how to surf, but the black girl tendencies got the better of me. All I could hear was my subconscious diva saying, "Beware that weave, child. Do not forget where you come from."

I also noticed that when I was not looking Gabe stared at me in a way that sent chills down my spine. It was very early to say anything on the matter, but his left eye grew smaller and his right fist clenched like he was doing everything in his power to not touch me. We spent more time than we had planned at the beach and only remembered to eat hours later.

"I am so sorry," Gabe started, but I stopped him. I did not care about my growling now stomach, not even that my weave was DONE and had to go. I had even forgotten how self-conscious I had felt when we started. All I cared about was how he made the moon sing when he said my name, and how I shivered whenever we touched.

"I will not make this easy on you. I am very hungry, but I had fun, so much fun that I forgot about lunch altogether." And as we lay there holding hands and munching on mint biscuits, I knew that somewhere very deep in my soul the darkness was leaving, and the universe was allowing me to smile again.

"We should go get something to eat."

"It's 10'o clock at night and the only places that are open at this time are the clubs and the Emergency Room and I'm not dressed for either," I said trying to reassure him about what he thought was a mess of a date. So we sat there all night talking about our undeniable love for photography and laughing at the fact that he used to have cornrows, and that I had fallen flat on my face the first time I wore my mother's heels (don't judge, they were five sizes too big), but then it became too cold and I remembered that I had to wash my hair… my own hair.

"Thank you for today," I said, as I stood in front of my room and waited restlessly for him to kiss me.

"Can I kiss you?" he asked, after what seemed like a long while.

"I thought you would never ask," I responded, bending my head to the side.

CHAPTER 6

How come black women are conditioned for marriage?

I want to understand why black women are encouraged to aim for marriage and are frowned upon when they choose a successful career over the idea of a family.

I stared at the sentence in front of me and wondered how I would continue the essay without sounding like an angry black woman. Yes, these days when you're black, a woman, have opinions, and you stand up for what you believe in, you're labeled as angry.

I was spending the night alone in my room because Zee was over at Gabe's. I tried not to think about the number of times she's let me down and canceled our bonding sessions over the last three months. She had a boyfriend, and I didn't. I had hook-ups and was fine with avoiding attachments, had no chance of being heartbroken, and no desire to be tied down. I probably sound like a crazy feminist - because I've been told this before, but I don't believe I need a man like I would a handbag or my freedom. As Warsan Shire puts it, "you cannot build homes out of human beings."

It is high time that society rejects this culture of making women feel less womanly for being successful, hardworking, and ambitious. Being a woman is not a maths problem that can be solved by adding a man and a submissive attitude to the equation. Being a woman shouldn't be about your ability to be led or fill a particular role. Being a woman shouldn't be about the size of your body. Womanhood shouldn't be frowned upon because even the late James Brown had it right when he sang "this is a man's world, but it wouldn't be nothing without a woman or a girl." Yes, we run the world, the homes, and the corporate workforce, and it's about high time that society accepted this fact, because we have.

I closed my laptop and smiled. I had 128 more words of the 2000 words I needed for my Constitutional Law essay on the Rights and Equality of Women. I had never suffered this much writer's block in my academic career. The words would normally be overflowing, typing effortlessly like I was possessed; but my talk with Zee has had me feeling insecure.

I love Zee, make no mistake, but then I also needed people in my circle that I could trust. I couldn't exactly trust someone who didn't even believe that her blackness was not beautiful unless it was tainted by a bit of whiteness now, could I? We were both running in different lanes, with different visions and although I could force myself to tolerate her decisions, I didn't have to compromise myself in the name of friendship. I was Moon Mosiapoa - since when do I compromise myself?

An hour later I was walking down Long Street heading to one of the most exclusive, most expensive restaurants to have lunch with my mother who had flown in from Johannesburg for some business involving charity work she was involved in with a couple of boys from Khayelitsha. I was excited, my mother would know what to say about this dilemma; plus it had been an entire month since I had last seen her.

I walked in and saw the beautiful woman I knew only as my mom sitting poised like a queen. She was regal, and everyone in the room recognized that.

"Hey, mommy!" I shrieked and bent down to kiss her. "How was the flight?"

"Long," Mathapelo replied, ordering more coffee.

"I hope the meeting went well though," I said and asked the waitress for an iced tea and the menu.

"It did." She avoided getting distracted, "Sorry love, but how was your day? I missed you, my baby."

"It was okay, I sent the proposal to the Vice-Chancellor for Steve Biko Day to be incorporated as an official school holiday, and I was re-elected as chair of the Golden Key Society. My application to host a radio slot was approved so I will be hosting the Politricks show on Friday evenings between six and eight. It's so exciting."

"Wow, I'm proud of you. I just hope your schoolwork, which is the priority, is not suffering with all these extra activities."

"Not at all, moms. I have a tutor for the modules giving me challenges," I said, trying to hide a smile.

I just didn't divulge that the tutor, Tokgamo Modise, also filled in as my hook-up when circumstances allowed. We had amazing chemistry and he wasn't intimidated by all the craziness in my head. Besides, it had only been five weeks and there were no signs of strings getting attached, which was so refreshing.

Lord, was he hot, and extremely intelligent, and did things to my body that I didn't think could be done before. He read my body like a poem and broke bones I didn't know were there. It was like he had turned me into an overnight gymnast. He was also a final year law student, and conscious. He had written an essay titled "The Modern Black Man," which was used as a reader by first- and second-year students.

"Good so how is Zee, and do you at least have a boyfriend?" Mathapelo asked, her eyebrows raised.

"Zee is fine... And, no!" I recoiled. I was not having the boyfriend talk with my mother despite her bringing it up every time we met.

"You worry me sometimes," She said, and I recognized her tone.

"Mom, don't start!" I wished the food would come already and decided to change the topic. "So what is the project about? You never told me."

But my mother took longer than usual to respond. I could see her face swell with emotion.

"I lied about that. I'm not here on any charity work."

"But your assistant said..." I stopped mid-sentence, confused about my mother lying.

"I told her to lie to you too," she intercepted, and I wondered when she got this good at keeping a straight face. She must be listening to a lot of Gaga while I'm away from home.

"Okay, I don't understand." I wanted to laugh but my throat lumped.

"I received a letter from this boy a couple of months back and didn't want to tell you anything until I had sorted it out myself."

“Sort what out?” My mother was dragging the conversation, making this out to be more exaggerated than it needed to be. I was anxious.

Mathapelo simply took a paper out from her purse and passed it across the table. I quickly opened it and started reading.

“My name is Bakang Lebakeng. My mother, Joyce Lebakeng died when I was five and I was raised by my grandmother. I never knew my father because no one ever talked about him, but he must have hurt my mother because she hated him. We struggled to make ends meet, and had two fatherless children surviving on practically no income. The pensioner’s allowance did not help much. I had to drop out of school to work in the town of Rustenburg, and now that my grandmother is sick. I need whatever help I can get.”

“He wants us, the organization, to give him money?” I asked confused but feeling for the boy. I couldn’t even begin to imagine how he could have survived living that way.

“Read on,” Mathapelo encouraged, then sipped her coffee.

“I recently found out from my grandmother that my father’s name was Bakang Mosiapoa.”

And in that instant, I went cold. I forgot that I was hungry and how much I had missed my beloved mother. What did this even mean?

“You mean dad had a love child?” I asked, but the idea was too horrific to comprehend.

“Something like that,” my mother answered nonchalantly, although I noticed that her hands were shaking.

"Well, he is lying. I don't believe it for a second. How could you even fall for this, Ma? People lie all the time. Things like this always come up." I stood up to leave, fuming. And although I wanted to have a nice lunch with my mother, I lost my appetite and did not want to be in the same space with her.

I dialed the first number I could think of. He answered on the second ring.

"Hey, I was just thinking about you."

"Where are you? What are you doing?"

"I'm in my room. Are you okay? You sound..."

"I'll be there in fifteen."

I needed to be in a familiar space. Somewhere I could be vulnerable, even for a moment, and not have to worry about who was watching. It was hard being strong all the time because people love it when you fall, it makes them feel good that they are one step closer to being on the same level as you. He never let me feel that way.

"Hey..." he said immediately as he opened the door, but I was not in the mood for formalities. I wanted to forget myself for the next few moments, and indulge in everything that might happen next. This was me being selfish.

CHAPTER 7

Inherited family traumas, coffee and poetry

I'm unsuccessful when it comes to relationships, and it's largely because I get the most ridiculous offers from guys. For a black-white girl, you're probably thinking that my Kim Kardashian ass and my Pearl Thusi hair, and my Michael Early eyes would speak for themselves but that's not the case.

I remember the first guy I had a crush on telling me that he was only dating me because I was half-white. To his friends, it would be a score and a half. The next time I liked someone, I was met with comments about how exotic I looked and how westernized I was. My friends had organized a blind date for me, and he sighed as he explained that I wasn't as rowdy or loud as black girls were. Of course, I was gobsmacked. Yet, I sucked it up and added a layer to my already thick, made that way by the many other racial slurs that had come my way.

What I refused to take was the first white guy I dated commenting on my ass being bigger than my boobs (a no-no in the white community). I exploded! Who did he think he was to tell me what I should look like? His simple response was that he wasn't surprised that I was acting out, all black girls are angry when it comes to love. Yes, he had the nerves, and I was at my wit's end, but I forgave him for being naive and ignorant and went back to the drawing board.

What was I missing? Was I too black where I had to be white or was I too white where I had to be black enough for my black brothers? People fail to understand my struggles, but when the only guy to ever offer the acceptance you need was someone you met on a social network at sixteen, it's less a struggle and more a war. The good news is that I am a hopeless romantic. The bad news is that I am starting to question my sexuality.

"Melisa!"

My mom is calling from the kitchen. I jump from my seat and close my laptop, forgetting to save my work. You know it's real when black call you by your full name. Normally, on a good day, it's "baby", "nana", "Lisa", or "Melly", and my experience has taught me the difference. I know to pray to the ancestors to save me from whatever punishment awaits me.

"Melisa!!"

"I'm coming, mom," but I take a couple of seconds to visualize an escape route. Did I leave the stove on? Did she find something in my pocket? Wait, what was I supposed to do?

I know, from my many years of living, that my two families are different from each other in ways other than the color of their skin. While my black family slaughters animals every chance they get, celebrating everything from new-born babies to death - the white side is big on diets, eating healthy, and campaigning for animal welfare, and the only time they celebrate is when someone gets engaged, the night before the wedding and the divorce party.

In my black family, you call everyone by their relation to you (aunt, grandma, or cousin), whereas we call each other by name on the white side. It hurt my feelings once when Claire referred to me as her half-sister. I mean, does it matter that we don't share both parents? Couldn't I just be her sister? Not half anything.

I'm not trying to paint the McFarland's black. I'm one of them. Yet, no halves are added to my title when I'm with the Ntungo's, even my stepdad calls me his daughter and treats me like I'm his own. I can't say the same for my stepmom though, while my siblings call her mom (as they should), I have to call her by name. Welcome to my world!

I get to the sitting room, where my mother is sitting watching the repeat of Khumbul'ekhaya; calm like she's not about to wage a war. The thing about black parents is that you never know what to expect from them. I swear, there is nothing worse than having someone spontaneously change on you, like a chameleon, but my mom will smile with you one second, and scream at you the next. You always have to be prepared... yet right now, I don't know why, but I can't read what's going on.

"Mama, you called?" I say, softly.

She ignores me and continues watching the reunion of some man with his mother who left with people she didn't know 25 years ago. I think it's ridiculous, but my mother sniffs, stifling a tear. I don't understand why people are touched by this.

"Mama..." I say again.

She doesn't look at me, but demands, "Give me the remote!"

And there we are, my mother, the amazing woman who gave birth to me has called me to the sitting room just to ask that I give her the remote that is lying next to her. I know you might find this impossible to believe, but trust me this lady has spent most of my life proving the impossible to be possible. Black parents do that, and if you dare mention the obvious, you're a rude, lazy, ungrateful child. They are as passionate about their Tupperware. There are two rules: don't call it plastic, and (if you look forward to a long and fruitful life) don't lose it.

I do as I'm told, give my mother the remote that is right next to her, and bite my tongue as I turn to walk away. But I don't get far before she asks me to bring her a glass of water. Wait, did I say "asks"? I meant "instructs". Black parents don't ask, they believe they are entitled to boss you around, and if you complain...

"I carried you for nine months. I never complained; and I have clothed you, fed you, and made sure you had all that you ever needed, and this is how you thank me? I don't know what I did to deserve this. Just look at MaKhumalo's daughter, she is well-mannered. Why can't you be like her Melisa?"

The comparisons used to bother me, but then I realized that she does it with everyone.

"Sibahle, I carried you for nine months, and never once did I complain. I have clothed you, fed you, and given you all that you've ever wanted. Do you know how many children don't get Christmas clothes but I buy them for you every year, and this is how you thank me? Why can't you be like MaNgwenya's daughter and listen to me?"

To which my thirteen-year-old sister would roll her eyes and put on her headphones. I tremendously envied her resilience. My fifteen-year-old brother was no different. He would go around mumbling under his breath, uttering obscenities that my mother wasn't supposed to hear.

"Kodwa Mxolisi, why don't you do as you're told? Is it difficult to pick up after yourself? I carried you for nine months and never once complained. I have clothed you, fed you, and made sure you were better than most children. Why can't you be like your cousin or your friend who is always doing as asked? Is this the thanks that I get from you? Tyhini!"

If we thought that we were the only ones who were on the receiving end of my mother's wrath, we were mistaken. Baba was also privy to it. "Maar Amos why can't you let me have what I want for just this once? I spent my time cooking for you, cleaning, and washing your clothes, and all I am asking is that you show some appreciation, or at least allow me to buy that fridge uSylvia has. Everyone in this house gets what they want, but I can't get anything for myself. Is this the thanks I get?" At this point, my stepdad would increase the TV volume and ignore her ranting. My mother even complained about who watched TV the most. Black parents!

That first white boy I dated... Remember him? Well, I should applaud him for not only being a model for what I wanted in a guy, but for also schooling me on what I did not want in a guy. I may have never actually kissed a boy before playing my first game of Spin the Bottle at an art camp when I was eighteen, but I was aware then of what I needed, first as a human being and secondly as a girl. I did not want to hear the word "half". Half-commitment, half-convinced, half-truth, half-evolved, half-respect, half-love, half-black, half-white...

I knew, despite what people said, that I wanted to be wanted, and that may seem selfish but there's nothing romantic about loving someone who wouldn't love you back. I also knew that just because you had two sets of parents who are happily in love was no guarantee that you'd end up with a fairy-tale ending. I cried whenever I watched *The Notebook* or saw a beautiful painting by any artist, even if I was generally not a fan of his work.

I went to church every Sunday to pray for life, for fame, for world peace, and sometimes I went ahead and prayed for love. I had just turned 21 and wanted to understand why I was still single with minimal hope of meeting someone special at this prime age when people around me were getting married, having children, and signing checks.

"Maybe instead of being so eager to save someone, you need to save yourself first," Sibahle said as we lay in bed talking about my predicament. I turned to her and smiled.

"When did you get so smart?" she may have been right, I don't know, but she was understanding.

"I don't know. When did you get so dumb?" She replied proudly.

CHAPTER 8

Don't go asking around

My father enjoyed telling me about the day he was arrested for transporting a grenade from Botswana to the uMkhonto we Sizwe underground base in Mahikeng. The story made his face come alive with pride. People wouldn't normally celebrate being arrested and detained by the white supremacist ruling party that believed in segregation and terrorizing powerless black people, but my father did.

He let me sit on his lap and play with his beard. His tobacco breath didn't intimidate and neither did his chocolate skin or his Tony Kgoroge features. My father was perfect. He was a hero according to my five-year-old self, and nothing (not even my mom calling from downstairs for me to go brush my teeth and go to bed) could take away the wide smile on my face, even with my front teeth missing.

I may not have understood it all but, while my friends enjoyed Winnie the Pooh and Beauty and the Beast, I was already reading books by Harper Lee and Robert Sobukwe at that age. To me, the beast was anyone who dared stand in front of me and make me question my relevance as a black person in the 20th century... Anyone who regarded me as an animal and believed I was not good enough. The beast was the oppressor, and I was going to do everything in my power to destroy that sense of thinking. I was my father's daughter after all.

While children my age dreamt of being like Barbie and were indoctrinated into the idea of a prince charming, a castle, and a happy ending, I was quoting Thomas Sankara and W.E.B. Du Bois. I knew from an early age that "a system cannot fail those it was never designed to protect," and that the black man was on his own, that we cannot stay silent when we are the ones destroying ourselves. I made that last one up, so don't bother googling it.

So, I pledged allegiance to the struggle and vowed that I would never allow myself Baks Mosiapoa's daughter, to be treated as mediocre because of the color of my skin. I knew that I would be spending every second of my life working twice as hard to be considered to be anything like my white counterpart.

"I was driving into the country under a false identity..."

"What is identity daddy?" I asked between yawns, my thumb in my mouth.

"Identity is something that shows who you are. Like a name."

"Why? Didn't you like your name?" I yawned again, dozily, trying hard not to miss the end of this story.

"No, I did like my name, but I couldn't use my real name."

"Why, Papa?"

"Because I had done things and I needed to be someone else so they wouldn't catch me."

My mom would choose that exact moment, as the story was getting interesting to come in and take me to bed. "Come baby it's time for bed. You will cajole with your father again tomorrow. Baks, let go of the child."

I tried to wriggle out of my mother's grasp but my body was too tired to fight. I needed one more minute and I'd hear how they caught my father, but Mathapelo Khama-Mosiapoa was having none of it.

"If you want to be a lady, you need your beauty sleep. You will listen to your father's storytelling again tomorrow." And that was the end of it.

I would wake up very early the next day to hear how the story ends and would find my father looking out the balcony, smoking a cigarette. He loved the view from his bedroom and said it reminded him of everything he had been through to be able to share this with his family. Seeing my father looking rested and serene made me happy too and I stood quietly by the door, not moving a muscle to avoid distracting him. Those were the best days, long before cancer attacked and made him limp and miserable - nothing like my hero.

"Do you want to hear how the story ends?"

"Yes, Papa."

"When you come back from school. You do know how important your education is."

"Yes, papa." I'd run downstairs so that Pricilla could get me washed and ready for school. Pricilla was the lady that took care of me, especially when my parents were out of town. She had been living with us for as long as I could remember and in the words of my mother, she was a godsend. I know though that there was nothing holy about Pricilla, trust me (unless the gods were punishing me).

While my mother and father let me get away with a lot of things, Pricilla didn't play that game. She'd say, in her deep and raspy voice, "Moon, I am going to talk to you once. The next time it's the back of my hand that's going to do the talking." I would do exactly as I was told. Yet, despite her being a killjoy most of the time, she was like a third mother to me and I loved her deeply.

She wasn't just the maid or helper who worked at our house, picking up after everyone; she is the reason I know how to tie my shoelaces, can sing the national anthem, and give basic responses in four languages. She would chase me around the house whenever I refused to finish my food. "There are children who die because they don't even have this thing that you call cornflakes. Come finish your food and don't be ungrateful."

She would throw shoes at me. I would laugh and run to my father hoping he would at least protect me from her, but he wouldn't. He would hide me for a second until Pricilla had calmed down but still insist I go finish my food. Having Pricilla around is one of the best memories from my childhood and the fact that her English was not as prim and proper as my parents made me aware of the privileges I had... and frustrated at the fact that black people don't have it easy in their own country. I was determined to change that.

"So, how long were you arrested for Papa?" I'd ask again, the childish curiosity getting the better of me.

"Which arrest are you referring to?" he replied and smiled. Despite what my father went through he still managed to find humor in the little things. I did a history project on our unsung heroes when I was twelve, and it came as no surprise to those who knew me that my father was the topic of my project.

"The one where you ended up going to Robben Island."

"Three years. I spent three years moving between Pollsmoor, Kroonstad, and then ended up on Robben Island. Those were the darkest years of my life, and the worst was not knowing... not knowing whether I would end up like Robert Sobukwe, thrown from the sixteenth floor, or if I would be beaten to death like Steven, or if I would receive a parcel bomb like Tiro. I did not know if I would ever get out. I had just met your mom on my last trip to Botswana and from the moment I laid eyes on her, I knew that she would be the one to hold me down."

"But mom said you met her before that."

"Your mom doesn't have an eye for detail." And to this, we'd burst out laughing.

Those were the best days... when my father wasn't waking up traumatized by the demons in his nightmares, crying and sweating. I knew deep down that my father had to have been angry, but he had played his part (even suffered for it) and having him alive was all we could ask for.

The physical were the scars worst. He had one right under his chin, which looked like someone had tried to slit his throat. His right finger was slightly bent as a result of torture, and he had one working kidney. I had to stop myself many times from cussing over what they'd done to him, but what kept me sane was how he embraced his freedom, how he was a conscious black man in the new South Africa.

My father never forgot where he came from, and he treated every black person he met with the same amount of respect as his wealthy counterparts. People appreciated him, and those who didn't have lived in his shadow. He was unapologetic about his beliefs. "From the second a black child is born they are already subjected to two struggles: being black and being isolated. His choices are to rebel against the system and live a life of crime; embrace the discourse that is designed to keep him perpetually oblivious to the opportunities available to him and spend the rest of his life mumbling "yes baas"... "no baas"; or he can create his own culture and be informed by black consciousness. There are only a few of those that fall into the last category, my baby, and I was determined to be one of them."

Pricilla would then kill the spell his words had cast on me, calling me to pick up the socks I had left lying on the bathroom floor. I would grunt and roll my eyes, but then my father would look at me with softness in his own eyes, and I knew that I had to start small if I wanted to be great. Which ironically is what my mother always said.

CHAPTER 9

I love you's sometimes come in threes

The first time Gabe said that he loved me we were lying on the grass outside watching the night skies. He lifted my chin, looked me straight in the eyes, and said the three magic words every girl wants to hear. He said slowly and I swear I felt my heart make a somersault. I closed my eyes and moved closer to hug my body against his. He was warm all over.

"Mhmm," I said half-heartedly because I didn't want him to feel pressurised. I wanted to hear those words, but I was hoping that when he said them he was serious about what he meant because Lord knows I believe in those words.

"Hey... hey... look at me. Open your eyes." I did and tried a smile but it didn't reach my eyes. All I could think of was that this guy with the grey eyes and a beauty spot on his forehead had said he loved me.

"You don't have to say it back. I just wanted you to know."

Yes, you just wanted me to know after three months of dating. Good one! I closed my eyes again and listened to his heartbeat.

The second time Gabe said he loved me, I was grinning like an idiot waiting for him to tell me what he thought of his birthday present. A weekend getaway that included surfing, bungee jumping, rock climbing, and melting marshmallows by the fire. I had saved up enough to give him a present he would like, and I needed him to love it. I wasn't an outdoor type of girl because you can't be sweating all day when you have a 16-inch weave and stiletto-shaped acrylic nails that hurt like hell when they break to worry about.

"Come tell me what you think!" I insisted, forcing him to wake up. His beautiful eyes were groggy and his hair was pointing in all directions as he leaned in for a kiss, but I moved away.

"No, please look and tell me what you think. I'm excited! Hella nervous too."

"Babe I told you not to get me anything." He pouted and rubbed his eyes.

I shook my head vehemently. "Seriously, that's like me telling you I am fine when I am not. Go on, open it. It's just a card."

"Okay, okay if you insist." The shock on his face when he opened it was of happiness. The gorgeous smile that appeared on his face was all I needed to see to know that he approved. My inner diva high-fived herself. I hated giving out presents because you could never know whether people would like them, but I had done well for a first-time gifter. This was his very first present from me.

"I… I… I love it," he managed to say after what seemed like forever.

"I know," I replied and clapped my hands together, "now you can go back to sleep."

"I love you," he said slowly again but was met with the same type of deadpan response as he had the first time he said it. My heart did the stupid dance again, and I knew somewhere deep down inside that I was irrevocably, insanely, and intensely in love with Gabriel Keogh III. I did.

"No..." I started, but felt overcome by emotions, "I love you." When he kissed me his mouth still tasted of sleep and his grey eyes pierced through my soul, I sang the alphabet in three languages. Today marks a year and three months since we've been together, and it cannot get any better than this. It's not easy, we still get rude comments from people when we walk into a restaurant holding hands or when we post a somewhat intimate picture on social media.

Although impossible to believe, some of our friends have slithered away because they find it uncomfortable to deal with us. It might be a race issue but, believe it or not, it doesn't bother us. We're totally oblivious to being "top deck", as we're often referred to. He is still the guy I fell for - with a perfect smile, intense grey eyes, and a body to die for - and I'm just the girl that makes him laugh and listens to him play morose love songs on his guitar without judgment (although he doesn't want to admit that I sing better).

"Why did it take you so long to tell me you love me?" Gabe randomly asks while we're lying in each other's sweat. I lift an eyebrow and give him the look.

"Seriously babe, are we going to argue about who said I love you first?" I know I am stalling. I can't just come out and tell him that I was crippled by fear, but continuing to be emotionally closed off it might have caused me to lose him.

"No, please... It's just... after I said it the first time... I thought you didn't feel the same way about me."

"Ha-ha! That's insane."

"So, why?" And that one question tugged at my heartstrings. It was now or never.

"The first guy I dated was my first love. We dated for almost four years and it was amazing. We were perfect for each other, and I could already see my tomorrow, the next couple of next years, and my whole future… a home, kids, and just pure bliss. It was supposed to work out, you know. We were like Bonnie and Clyde, and everyone would say that we were made for each other, that we belonged together.

"I went through a lot of firsts with him. He was the first guy I kissed, the first guy I had sex with, and my naive thought that it was going to last forever." I stop to see if I am boring him, but Gabe is listening attentively. More focused than I have ever seen him. I smile.

"And for a long while afterward I made myself believe that he loved me too. I needed to hang onto that, or I would have been destroyed. I cried for months on end after it ended. I couldn't eat or sleep. I was an emotional mess. I stalked him, his family, his friends, and his new girl. I needed to know why he had chosen someone over me. You know, like was she prettier than me? Was she smarter? How did she laugh? Was he happier with her? I thought if someone could leave you after four years then what's to stop them from leaving you at all? I stayed indoors and cried every day until my older sister told me to stop it and forced me to deal with the fact that I had done all I could to love him. It just wasn't meant to be. I prayed, went to church, and gained some weight after some time. Then I saw them together some time after. She was pregnant. Instead of crying I hugged her and wished them well."

Gabe is still quiet, and I can hear him breathing heavily.

"Why?"

"Because I believe in love, babe. I'm a hopeless romantic and even after feeling like my heart had been ripped out of my chest, I still wanted to fall in love. I knew I had to forgive to heal and be able to feel that love again with someone else."

We then lie in each other's arms, silent, listening to our hearts beat simultaneously. We stay this way for a long while, and then it occurs to me that he may not be able to handle my baggage. From my experience, a year and three months could after all mean nothing. I twiddle my thumbs and bite my tongue. I went ahead and opened myself to him and now feel extremely vulnerable.

"It's crazy because everyone believes that black women cannot love because they are all angry from having been hurt, but to hear you say this and still love me like I am the only guy you have been with is amazing. You keep surprising me."

I exhale deeply, smile, and feel my heart get lighter. "Oh, we're playing the race card now?" I tease and Gabe tickles me.

"Gabe stoooooooooop!" and I wiggle out of his warm embrace which feels like home. We go on to stuff our faces with takeaway Chinese noodles and red wine, and while the drink makes my baby sleepy, I must admit though that it makes me excited in a way that I need him to participate in. I watch him fall asleep, and his hair falling on his face makes me aware that he is due for a haircut.

One thing about me is that I am unapologetic about being a hopeless romantic. I believe I have so much love to give. I still believe that there are people with good intentions despite the world being a cold and dark place.

My parents have been married for almost thirty years and they still inspire me. It's refreshing to see my older siblings also subscribe to the institution of marriage. My sister Namhla has been married for more than five years and my brothers, Sizwe and Mthunzi, are also heading very successful marriages. I've always enjoyed how we're all present at family gatherings and the feeling of love is abounds.

I believe that love sees no color, even though Gabe and I will always have to tiptoe around people who see race even when the lights are off, and those who make jokes about people who throw side comments at us. Yes, we're different (we will always be) but for as long as his kisses leave me senseless, we will continue starring into each other's eyes as though the secret to infinity written within.

I can handle girls calling me names and friends no longer inviting us to parties for as long as the love that lives in our hearts transcends color. I can handle anything because this is the kind of love I live for.

He says, "I love how you laugh," and every part of my body goes into reverse. So enchanted that I need an atlas to know where I am going.

CHAPTER 10

Don't forget the SPF when life comes for your child

I use sunscreen. I know you're probably wondering why this is relevant, but I'm merely stating the fact. I know from experience that most black people don't see the necessity of protecting themselves from the sun but since I'm white I have no choice. My maternal grandmother would give me a sideway glance each time I asked her to put sunscreen all over my face and arms just before I went out to play with the other kids.

"Haai Mlisa (she somehow manages to pronounce my name in the most African way possible), yintoni lento?"

"It's sunscreen, Gogo," my preteen self explained, eager to go play house with the neighborhood kids. Manelisi, the local bully, always managed to play the father for some reason. The snotty diva, Chichi, would play his wife and I would always be the madam. I didn't understand the racial innuendo till I was twelve and watching *Madam & Eve*. My being fair-skinned meant to them that I didn't belong in their community. I couldn't even be the annoying neighbor, although I felt that I could have done a better job than Unathi. It hurt me somehow.

"Ndizokwenza nton ngayo keh?" she asked with the same kind of attitude and tone my mom had inherited from her. I rolled my eyes, and this was my first mistake.

"I can't go outside without sunscreen. Daddy says the sun will give me cancer." My second mistake was mentioning my father in her presence. She went off.

"Oh, so utatakho thinks you're better than us? Huh? How come we all go outside, and we don't have le cancer yakho? kodwa asi'sebenzisi le sunscream yakho? Haai suka maan hamba uyodlala." And that would be the end of it.

If Mkhulu was around he would diligently rub it over my body while telling me that I was special. I loved those moments, but Gogo Khesiwe didn't allow such greatness to rule our lives. I didn't judge her because she didn't know any better. Scientifically, my skin was bound to be affected by the sun because I had less melanin than the black children I played with in the neighborhood. I had a higher chance of contracting skin cancer than they did. Also, I couldn't just jump into the river and swim in the dirty water like the other children did, even though I knew how to swim by the time I was four and a half. This had nothing to do with pigmentation, but I used it as an excuse regardless. I just found it gross.

Grandma also didn't understand why I was lactose intolerant. To her, no black child could be allergic to milk. She would walk around the house making loud remarks aloud and asking questions that she didn't want answers to.

"Haai ke Mlisa imihlolo lena. Ngumntu otheni onganxili amasi? Kodwa lomntana KaNokuzola unamaqhinga. So what will you eat... Sushi?"

Despite my troubles with being a white child in a black family... I loved visiting the Eastern Cape so much that I learned to grow a thick skin. Ironically, looked forward to running after the chickens and learning to milk the cows with my grandfather, and whenever I felt like crying I would remember his wise words "strong walls shake but they never collapse."

I was fifteen and a half when dad coughed up enough courage to talk to me about the birds and the bees, but somewhere along it got so awkward that he left it and asked my stepmother to step in. I was so confused when he started mentioning sex, and I found it funny because it was the first time outside of school I had heard any adult use the word we read about in the blue-and-white Life Orientation textbook.

Of course, my mom just used the most intimidating voice to tell me that sex was bad. "Don't you dare open your legs and have children, Melisa, and don't believe any boy that tells you he loves you, they just want to sleep with you, and then they'll leave you."

So, I put my defenses on, stayed indoors, and ran away when boys asked me my name, and that is why I am still a virgin at 22. I guess I was more scared of what my mother would do to me than curious about what a boy could do between my legs that I kept myself completely closed off. The idea of her possibly chasing me with a broom in the middle of the street terrified me more than the idea of disappointing her by getting myself knocked up.

I was embarrassed when dad came up to my room on one the weekends I spent with him and asked if I had a boyfriend. Looking down, I answered, "No daddy," and he was ever so kind and gentle.

"Don't be shy, it's perfectly normal for anyone your age to be seeing someone."

Not from where I came from. "Mom would kill me," I said.

That was only half the truth though. She would cut me up into tiny pieces, carve the letter A into my forehead, and burn me alive. She'd then continue to pour acid over the ashes just to make sure that I had no way of even making it to the afterlife. I wasn't exaggerating.

I felt dad take a deep breath, probably wondering how he got himself into this mess with my mother to begin with.

"Is there someone you like?"

I felt my cheeks burn an embarrassing scarlet, "Yes, but he doesn't like me."

"How do you know? Have you asked him?" my father was clearly getting a kick out of this awkwardness. I looked up at him sharply, where did he think we lived? Girls don't ask guys out where I came from, it's taboo.

I shook my head, "No, I'm a lady," and tried to stay sane, "plus mom says boys just want to get between my legs and leave me with a baby and some disease." This left him shocked and expressionless for a while. I did a victory lap around the room.

"Oh, okay... that's... that's, uhm... okay... let's... I, uhm... let me call your stepmom, she might be better at this. You know, with her being a woman and all."

And that was the last time my father tried being the cool dad and talking about sex with me. It was a courageous effort, and for that I must give him credit, but when all you've been taught is that sex is a sin and it's dirty, and you need to wait for marriage to have it, you struggle to express yourself sexually because you expect the Lord to be watching, and you unwillingly begin to believe that it could be true.

Although my white family was expressive with their love and affection and found it nothing to be ashamed of, my black family shied away from this. I can tell you honestly that my father and stepmom kiss and hold hands, and on a few occasions I've heard what sounded like people deep in the throngs of passion. Yet, not even when my stepfather got a promotion from work and mom cooked him his favourite meal do I remember them kissing, let alone holding hands. They didn't even sit on the same couch when they were watching soapies or the news. You could always feel the cold air between them.

I soon realized that in black culture emotions are reserved for funerals and winning the Lotto. Parents didn't encourage their children to express themselves and didn't want to hear anything about them being sexual and, to a large extend, that contributed to them being curious and secretly experimental. Condoms are bound to go missing, and someone will whisper, "trust me, baby, I know what I'm doing," in the dark.

Do you know that black communities amount for the highest rates of teenage pregnancy, unprotected sex and sexual experiments? Yet, if you dare say too loudly, you'll be called out for conspiring with the devil and being full of Satanism.

I am a Christian and believe in the Holy Trinity, but I've also seen the statistics and think we'd be singing a different tune if black parents were more open with their children about the consequences that came with participating in the act, and the children weren't left to read about sex from Playboy magazine and watch late night X-rated movies with the sound low.

I thank my mother for instilling the fear of God in because it prevented me becoming a statistic - but we are not all that lucky. I'm 22 years old, and many people don't believe it when I say that I'm still a virgin and I've never really had a boyfriend. I have had crushes, (serious ones for that matter), and have only been kissed once or twice.

The image in my mind of my mother chasing me with a broom in the middle of the street with devils' horns on her head is what has made me keep my legs super shut. I'm all kinds of brave but that's a war I'm not ready to start.

"You think they love you? No, my child, they love what they can get from you, and trust me they can get it from anyone else. So, don't you ever let them take it without paying for it? Let him marry you first. Or else, Melisa, I will kill you." I know she will.

CHAPTER 11

Wear your anger like a temporary skin

I don't believe there's a God. I always ask people who preach to me about their god, "where was your God during the more than 350 years when black people were being oppressed? Where was your God when the whites came to Africa and kidnapped our people to use as slaves? Where was your God when the Jews and blacks were being persecuted by the white Germans? Where was he when the Boers and British were enslaving our people and taking our lands, or when our fathers and brothers were being thrown from buildings and their homes were being run down by bulldozers? Where was he when black children suckled inequality from their mother's breasts? If he is indeed omnipresent and always on time, how come he let us suffer and die for all those years before finally coming to our rescue? Where was he, where was he when blacks like Saartje Baartman were being kept naked in zoos and black children were being treated like monkeys and fed bananas to entertain the white man?

On the day I told my mother I was not going to church anymore, she looked at me sternly and said, "you're coming Moon." I stubbornly stood by the door and asked her why.

"Because we need to give thanks to God."

"I don't have anything to be thankful for. I cannot worship someone who doesn't protect me when I need him to, someone who allows me to be treated like I'm inferior, and allows me to be torn from my mother's breast to go worship a white man who treats me like a slave. What am I thanking him for?"

My mother stood there shocked and didn't say a word. She knew she couldn't argue with me on this. I was an angry black child who needed to understand why I had to be loyal to a culture that had continued to oppress me for centuries. It's like Desmond Tutu said: "When the missionaries came to Africa they had the Bible and we had the land. They said 'Let us pray.' We closed our eyes. When we opened them we had the Bible and they had the land."

I wasn't going to fall into that trap, I was going to be an intellectual black person who believed in herself, her abilities, and the fact that the land was never the whites to take to begin with. I didn't hate the church, I was merely calling it out for all the questions I had that had never been answered.

My father also didn't go to church, and my being a daddy's girl meant that he was on my team. We'd stay behind and read books written by Patrice Lumumba and African writers like Chinua Achebe and Wole Soyinka and we would argue about whether there was an African renaissance brewing and the need to give birth to an African revolution that embodied black consciousness. I was only twelve years old but already a force to be reckoned with.

He would smoke his cigarettes and I liked believing that at that moment I was his right hand. There was nowhere I wanted to be other than next to him, breathing in his nicotine, and taking in the wisdom that went beyond the history books that taught about Jan van Riebeeck and the Groot Trek and nothing about how Shaka had created one of the strongest armies, how Sol Plaatje was the first person to translate the Bible into Setswana.

I learned about how uMam Ntsiki Mashalaba stuffed Biko's papers in her son's diapers when the white police came to terrorize them in the middle of the night. The baby had cried but the police never figured it out.

The only thing that stood between me and gaining wisdom from my father, drawing on his experiences, was aunty Pricilla. She was a nightmare and would interrupt us every chance she could. "Moon, come brush your teeth. Come eat your breakfast."

"I am not hungry."

"I didn't ask if you were hungry, child. Come eat your breakfast, some children don't even know what breakfast Is." Embarrassed by my privilege, I would rush through breakfast just so I could run back and listen to my father talk about his meeting with Chris Hani back in the 80s. But Pricilla would not stop.

"Moon, your lunch is ready... Come pick up your shoes... Why is the TV on?.. Did you do your homework?.. Moon, come take a bath... Leave your father, he's busy... Come eat supper... It's time to sleep... Moon..."

I'd sometimes stick cotton wool in my ears just so I wouldn't hear a thing she said. I couldn't complain to my mom because she loved Pricilla, and would just tell me to stop being silly and walk on by on her clacking heels, sipping tonic water as if what I had asked was irrelevant.

I didn't want to burden my father with my pity party, however, he was the Minister of Justice and had important work to do. He had dropped out of Law at Wits, but deserved a piece of the new government's pie. That's how I gained an interest in Law grew. I was adamant that I wanted to be a lawyer after matric. My mother thought that I was paying tribute to my deceased father because I loved him dearly, but being a lawyer was more a calling to fight for African people through the legal system than it was about making a name as Bakang Mosiapoa's daughter. A lot of Africans end up punished for crimes they did not commit because they cannot afford private lawyers. Accused who are unfortunate end up with an overworked state lawyer who is dispassionate about his work because of the caseload and associated pressures.

One may think it crazy but there was a case I came across where a girl was being accused of helping her boyfriend kill and dump his other girlfriend's body when she physically couldn't have done it. She wasn't mature enough, emotionally, to have pulled it off, and neither was she in the vicinity when the murder took place. She would have received a life sentence had my father not intervened in her case, and no one would have bothered to find out why she had been implicated in the first place. Welcome to the South Africa we live in!

"Where are you going?" Tokgamo asks alarmed and I roll my eyes.

"I have to go."

"You don't *have* to. You just don't want to stay."

"I always leave."

He tries to pull me back into bed, but I stand abruptly. "Not if I can help it," I laugh and lean against the wall. I have my jeans on, and I see my sneakers, but I cannot find my bra or my ANC t-shirt.

"Can I have my bra please," I beg, "I'm getting cold," my hands covering my nipples. He winks and tries to seduce me, and although I'm eager to leave, I find it cute and sexy.

"Come to bed and I will warm them up for you."

"It's after two, Tuks, I have to go."

After a minute of just staring at me, he bends over the side of the bed to retrieve my clothes and hands them to me. "You know you don't always have to run. I'm right here."

"I know that. Which is why I always call before I come over, in case you have someone."

"What do you mean someone… like another girl?"

"Yes, like another girl. Unless you are trying to tell me something."

He laughs and I capture the sound of his laughter in my head. It's something I always look forward to. His chortling, and the way his eyes dance when he is happy.

"No girl, I am not even thinking about that."

"So, I'll call you?"

"Yeah."

"Okay, bye."

And just as I am about to leave, Tokgamo pulls me closer to his face and whispers, as if possible for someone else besides us to hear what he has to say. My ears burn with the intensity of the words leaving his mouth.

"You know, it's just you. Not that it matters, but you have to do away with the stereotype that all black guys are players. Some of us can stay committed to a girl, even when she does not want us, and we're also into cuddling after sex."

CHAPTER 12

Who teaches her how to be a woman?

I have a better relationship with my black sister than I do with my white one. I won't start on how I relate with my brothers because Luke is ten and Mxolisi is an idiot. I know that you're thinking that I shouldn't compare my siblings because it's not fair, but I'm not. I love all of them dearly, but I'm just stating the obvious.

Sibahle is exactly like our mother... loud, vibrant, and proudly Xhosa. She also loves cooking and dances to indigenous songs with two left feet. She also does that thing of rolling her eyes exactly as mom does. They're so alike that people have stopped them on the street to ask if they're sisters, and you may think my mother would glow over the compliment, but you'd be wrong. She resents the comparison so much that she's come close to slapping innocent people for merely bringing it up.

"What do you mean are we sisters? What are you trying to say? Are you saying I don't look woman enough to be her mother?"

She once asked the guy if he was hitting on her or her 13-year-old daughter. "Do you think you're charming anyone of us?"

I swear I am not making this up. I have to always hide my face behind a magazine - to which she will also have something to say. "Melisa, why are you reading that magazine? Do you think that Kelly Khumalo reads about you when she wakes up? You don't concentrate as much on your school books... do you think those tabloid stories will come up in the exams?

Sibahle and I relate better because our mother doesn't allow dating, drinking, or missing church, so we're forced to stick with each other. Claire, on the other hand, has already had a sex talk with my father and stepmom. She is allowed to date as long as she brings the idiot over. Those are my father's words, not mine.

You see, we don't have much to bond over because my sister gets to have these kinds of privileges. She gets to have nuts in her breakfast, listens to punk rock, and likes making comments like "why is your hair so thick?" I mean, who does that? Don't get me wrong, we have a good relationship, but it is what it is... No fireworks or anniversaries. I'm 13, the same age as Sibahle, and I'm still trying to figure out which family is less complicated to live with.

My mother keeps saying that we act like the devil came down and matched up Sibahle and me. We share everything from shoes to bras, not boys though. My sister seems to have better luck with the boys - I should actually take notes. We both genuinely love our grandparents and get away with a lot of things with uTaMkhulu. Mxolisi hates having to herd cows and is always reluctant to go there.

His eye winking at us, uTaMkhulu often tells Sibahle that farm work was a man's job.

"I don't want to be a man," Mxolisi grumbles in response, but we all know better than to believe him. He may have grown up in the township but is a hot-blooded Xhosa male, and that means that he takes his manhood seriously.

"What happens in the bush TaMkhulu?" I asked him one day, curious to find out but also nervous about knowing.

"I can't tell you that my child," he replies, looking down at his half-empty cup of coffee. This is his way of saying "I don't want to tell you," but I need to know. The boy next door, uSabelo, was in the bushes last year and all of a sudden everyone treats him with respect and calls him "bhuti". It's like they forgot that he used to run around chasing young girls and steal my grandmother's chickens.

"Do they beat you up?"

"No, who told you that?"

"No one, uSabelo doesn't steal chickens like he used to, and he no longer swears."

He is aware of the confusion written all over my face, "They teach you how to be a man."

"Is it like school, where they give you books to read and tests to write?"

My grandfather takes a long sip of his coffee before answering, "Something like that." But I don't believe him, not even for a second; and so I go straight to the source and ask Sabelo himself. We grew up together and I figure he would just come right out and tell me. There should be nothing to hide, right?

I find him sitting under the tree at his house, a stick in his hand. "Hello, Sabelo." He doesn't reply, which I find odd. Yet,

I'm a white girl visiting her grandparents in the Eastern Cape. He probably finds me to be the odd one.

"What are you doing today? We are playing hide-and-seek later today. You want to come?"

"I don't play with children, Melisa. Hamba maan!" And he turns to look the other way.

I wasn't hearing any of it, and exploded, "Look here, Sabelo, it's not my problem that you had to spend time in the bush sleeping on some grass without electricity, okay? I don't understand what's gotten into you. We used to play together, and don't think I've forgotten how you used to steal my grandmother's chickens. In fact, I think I should tell her the truth."

I stand up angrily, my sunhat blowing in the warm breeze, and walk to my house. How dare he? Does he think I'd forget? Sabelo doesn't call me back to explain why he is acting like a pain in the ass or to say that he is sorry, despite my dramatic exit. He lets me be and I grow even angrier by the second, but I don't tell my grandmother about Sabelo stealing her chickens - Lord knows she would send him to a place worse than the bush.

Sabelo and I continued to grow apart until it was so awkward that we didn't talk at all. He had changed and my naive self didn't want to accept it. Years later I heard that he had gone to Cape Town to study medicine and his family wanted him to marry the mean girl Chichi. She was beautiful, no doubt, but was also the devil's advocate, and I couldn't understand what he saw in her.

Today I'm happy to say that I understand my tradition better. My brother is nearing the time when he'd also need to go to the bush. He is scared but has no choice but to go because it's a rite of passage and otherwise he will forever be cast out and treated like a boy. I am hoping that he will perhaps tell me what really happens up there - but I doubt it. I'll probably blog about it and people will want to know how I know, and they might just find out, and well… tradition is very complicated.

I'm sitting with Sibahle talking about this and how Mxolisi will probably be a bigger pain as a "man" than he already is. We laugh because the truth is, we know that a lot of our unanswered questions will forever remain a mystery. "Sisi, would you date a boy who hasn't gone to the bush?" Sibahle asks randomly. It's a weird question and one I haven't thought about before. I roll my eyes at her, but she is serious.

"Yes. I don't see why not." I answer honestly.

"I won't," and I can tell that she's being earnest.

"Why not?" Now, this I have to hear.

"Because most of my friends say he will not know how to do the things that men do. I don't want that."

It then hits me that although I'm caught between two very different worlds, I am still expected to fit in with both of them, but sometimes my white genes take over more than my black genes and I say things like "I don't care whether he had to be nipped in front of a bunch of people by an old man with failing eyesight and all he did was partake in stick fighting and chanting songs - if he buys me flowers, sends me good morning texts and calls me beautiful then that's all I want." Sibahle knows me like the back of her hand though, we're closer than conspiratorial Robbins.

"I think Sabelo likes you," she says to me one day as we wash Gogo Khesiwe's favorite dinner set.

"Please, Sabelo and I haven't spoken to each other in nine years."

"Who's counting?" she adds, laughing. I blush, and my cheeks glow a light shade of pink.

"Whatever! Besides, he's with Queen Chichi."

"Oh, please! Everyone knows that she's cheating on him."

"Well if he knows then why is he still with her?"

"Her family is rich, and she's using muthi on him." We both laugh.

Sibahle is like my mother, she exaggerates a lot. Sometimes I feel like they should have their own reality TV show.

"He's a doctor. I doubt he believes in that."

"Really, white girl? We are in the Eastern Cape, who doesn't believe in that?"

"I don't..."

"But you believe in ghosts. It's the same thing."

"No, it's not..."

"Whatever, he likes you and you're too much of a virgin to notice." Sibahle has this annoying habit of reminding me of how inexperienced I am when it comes to relationships. She's my sister, so she gets a free pass, but it's annoying nonetheless.

The best part of all of this is that she gets courted by almost every boy. I don't see her remaining single past the age of sixteen.

"Stop talking about me, what about you and that boy, Phiwe?" I know she thinks no one knows that she's been sneaking out to see him. "And why are you keeping it from me?"

"He won't be a boy much longer. He is going to the bush next year. You should draw a line in front of him with a stick. He should give you money." I laugh. I know Sibahle won't find it funny but why not amuse myself? True to her character my passionate little sister chases me around with a wet dishcloth. I scream but continue to torment her. "He is going to also be moody when he comes back. Maybe they will teach him not to love, or maybe you won't be woman enough for him. How will you kiss him with that red thing on his face? And remember you can't sleep with him? That would suck for your oversized breasts." I say and point at her frontal with a wicked grin. My baby sister is no longer a baby, it's scary and amazing all at the same time.

For me, culture has always been two-sided. While the only thing my father worried about was pizza on Wednesday nights and going to church on Sunday mornings, my mother threw salt around the house, burned *impepho* when anyone suffered from insomnia, and made us all say "please and thank you" as much as possible.

I was attracted to the charm that traditions possessed to the point where my curious mind created trouble for me with a lot of grownups. In my black family, you're not given room to ask questions that will ultimately make the other person uncomfortable or unable to give you an answer. It was decided, because of this, that when I turned seven my father would have full custody until I was able to make up my own mind; and in an instant my mother became the weekend parent.

It was okay for a while, and this is for lack of a better word… but we all know that a girl child needs her mother.

"I don't know where I fit in," I said once to a friend when she asked me which family I was most comfortable with. "With my dad, it's all black and white, nothing is confusing but it's harder for some reason with my mother. I feel like I always have to prove myself although, it's my heart that keeps me going back and you can never argue with the heart."

"Well, I guess it must be nice having very different parents."

"Yes, it is," I would lie because I hated the fact that people always made such comments. "My father gives me chocolate for dinner while my mother only rewards good behavior. Does that make sense? No? I thought so."

CHAPTER 13

There are no easy wins in the court of love

"Affirmative."

"Hearsay."

"Leading."

"Misleading."

"Hahaha."

"Why are you laughing? If they object you need to be able to think on your feet."

"No jokes hey, I didn't know."

"Your sarcasm can only take you so far."

"Says who?"

Raises eyebrow.

"Trust me it's worked well so far."

"That's because people relate to a pretty face."

"Can I object to bullshit in court?"

"Hahaha, now it's my turn to laugh."

"Which means I'm winning. Okay, I see a way to prosecute this case. The facts alone won't win you the verdict, so you need to play the man."

"I thought of that."

"And?"

"It's a racial case."

"Exactly and many people are oblivious to the current realities versus the structured society that we have all been led to believe exists and caters to the black man."

"Someone could argue that losing your temper has nothing to do with race, but when it's white on black we scream racism."

"Yes, but you can't plaster over a wound made by a machete. Eliminating the main issue that this man (regardless of the color of his skin) acted in a way that was discriminatory and treated them in a demeaning manner because he felt "insulted by his presence" has more to do with the man than with a dictionary definition of an act used to cover oppression."

"Still, someone could argue that racism isn't entirely the factor in every case unless people make it out to be, and the man could argue that he found himself in a predicament and acted in the only way that seemed reasonable under those circumstances?"

"Seriously Tuks, how can calling someone the k-word be reasonable?"

"It doesn't, but if he has a strong argument it could leave reasonable doubt... his privacy was being invaded."

"At a public place? Are you serious?"

"These are all the things that the opposition could throw at us if we are not prepared to look outside the boundaries of racism and deal with the invasion of privacy as well." Then he laughs, clearly refusing to believe that such ridiculousness could be used to weaken the case.

"I can't think. There is way too much idiocy in this case."

"I know babe."

"So do you expect to go about it?"

"I don't know yet but I'm looking at possible precedents tomorrow morning."

"If this is what fourth-year Law sounds like, I am not ready." I smile.

"You're more than ready. You have me as a teacher." He returns a sexy beam.

"Tutor, don't get over your head." I retaliate with a coy smirk.

"I thought you liked me using my head." He winks modestly.

"Which head are you referring to?"

"Oh, you want to know now…?" His hands grab at me.

"Ha-ha look at you." My heart is blissful.

"So are you staying the night?"

"No. you know I don't."

"It's got to change."

"Your head? No, I like them both."

"No yours."

"Please."

"Honestly, you're screwed the wrong way."

"Okay, I'll see you tomorrow. Should I order takeaways for tomorrow night?"

"Nope, I'm spending the night at the library."

"You didn't tell me that?"

"I just decided."

"Okay, bye."

And this is how we make it work. We meet up, make out, talk about work, and make out some more, thrash our brains, and I leave. I always leave and that's only recently started being a problem, just because I'm not addressing it doesn't mean I am oblivious to it.

I like Tokgamo. He is smart, poetic, and soulful. He has dark chocolate skin, an arrogant smile, and small eyes that hide beneath a bush of perfect eyebrows. His fingers are long and clean, and he smells of water and Hugo Boss on good days and Armani on better ones, and we complement each other. Yet, while everyone believed that I would be the one to fall in love with him first, I proved them wrong.

I don't do love. I am too practical and realistic to believe in illusions created to sponge off people's emotions. Do I like him? Yes, a lot. Do I care for him? Yes, I can be selfless to the point where I do things that will make him happy. Do I see us together in the near future? Maybe, if it works out all right. But for now, today, when I have all my limbs working together for a common goal and his voice still manages to make me forget my mother's warnings about losing beauty sleep over men... I'm good. I do not understand why not having a title for whatever it is that we have going should be a problem, or why not sleeping over should be a mood killer.

I get to my place and find Zee sleeping in. It's a miracle! "Hey, sleepyhead."

"Hey, ice queen. You ran away again?"

"I didn't run away from anything."

"You know, if I didn't know you any better I'd say that you're Cinderella. Come midnight you run away, leaving poor prince charming all bewitched and confused."

"I am. Ha-ha, my mother taught me to always come home before midnight."

"So how is lover cupid doing after shooting himself with his own arrow?"

"He's okay. He will be... He has a mock case to prep for and I have my first radio gig in the morning.

"Oh cool. Should I get wine for that?"

"No honey, didn't your mama teach you? You can't have just that without having something to eat."

"Ha-ha, Gabe also doesn't understand."

"Which reminds me... why are you home?"

"I live here."

"Right."

"I missed you."

"You did?"

"Funny..." But before we know it we're laughing at ridiculous videos of people who cannot walk in heels, how people still buy KFC regardless of the controversy surrounding the fast food chain, and the sad reality is that she and I might never get to break the internet like these people. I've missed this.

"So when is your mom coming to Cape Town again? You two make me so jealous when you're together," Zee asks, and even though the question is anything but innocent I cannot help that the hair on the back of my neck stands.

The last time my mother and I met it didn't end on a good note, and despite her best attempts at reconciliation by calling and texting, I'm not ready to deal with the fact that my father may have a mystery child that no one knows about; and if this is true, he could be the son he never had but always wanted. Basically, my replacement.

"Oh, I don't know. We are not really talking right now."

"What?" Zee asks and jumps out of bed in disbelief, her eyes wide open.

"Or rather, I'm not talking to her."

"What did you do?"

"Why does it have to be me?" I ask loudly and throw a pillow at her. How could she even assume that it was my fault? I'm very touched that someone I consider a friend would hold such accurate presumptions about me.

"Well because you are difficult to live with, Moon. I can't even tell when you are having a good day."

"I'm not," I reply indignantly.

"Oh yeah, then why do I have to hear from bigmouth Lerato that you have a boyfriend and not from the horse's mouth?"

"Because I do not date and you should know that, and Lerato is exactly what you called her, bigmouth," I answer and instinctively use my right hand to slowly rub the scar on my left hand. It has been there for a few years and this meaningless gesture is my way of ensuring that it is still there. I do it unconsciously sometimes, without intending to, and most times I'm oblivious to people around me noticing that I do it.

"Why do you always do that?" Zee asks drawing me back to the present. She nods her head at my hand, and I quickly throw my hands to my sides.

"What?" I ask trying to sound stupid so she can hopefully let the matter rest. This is not something I am willing to ever talk about.

"Don't play dumb Moon. You're doing it again," she continues and lets out a short laugh. "I know you don't like looking vulnerable to people but can you at least tell me who you're sleeping with? I am not going to judge you... and trust me, I'm more than thrilled that you're getting your cold heart warmed up once in a while."

"Go ask bigmouth Lerato," I suggest wickedly, throwing another pillow at my friend.

"That's not fair." Zee concedes, and I smile and stand up to walk across the room to where the bar fridge is. It's times like these when I feel like being a girl and indulging in some comfort food. Maybe we will have ice cream with sprinkles of laughter.

"I know it isn't, but I like our conversations better when we talk about your romantic liaisons with your boyfriend, who I don't like but tolerate. Where is he anyway?"

CHAPTER 14

God, I like this one

After a year with someone, you know whether you want to continue rubbing their back when they sprain a muscle and if you still want to make them soup when they are riddled with influenza. It had been a year and six months since I had been with Gabe, and I had an idea of whether or not I wanted to spend another year and six months with him. I had decided that it was time for him to officially meet my family.

My parents' 30th wedding anniversary was coming up and everyone was going to be there. I wanted them to meet the guy I had fallen intensely in love with. All geeky, he possessed out-of-this-world qualities and managed to not only stand out as if he was a Greek God but fit in like a beautiful star in the night sky. I was so genuinely and ridiculously happy that the ends of my lips burned from being overstretched when I smiled, but Gabe was so nervous that it seemed like his eyes would pop out of their sockets.

"So will your family like me?" he asked nervously, and I smiled at his uneasiness.

"What is there not to like? You're cute and you eat like a black boy. They'll definitely like you." I replied in mock honesty.

"No, I'm serious babe." His voice sounded unassured, even to himself.

"So am I. Look, my parents do not have a problem with you being white... I guess that's what you're worried about... as long as you love their daughter, buy me chocolate and still look at me like I am the only one that rocks your world, you are fine." This pretty much sums up every parent's worst nightmare.

"You know I only have eyes for you," he says softly and my heart lurches forward.

"How could you not?" I ask mockingly, my body temperature rising to an inferno.

I lied to Gabe for the first time. I did not tell him that it was my family he had to be on the lookout for, even though my parents would be fine. My parents would probably give him a hard time depending on whether they were hungry when we arrive. My brothers would be fine because I'm their little sister after all, and they must scare away any frogs and make sure that I end up with a great guy. It's also a male thing, I guess. My sister loved him from the second she heard how happy I sounded when we spoke on the phone. She had also been advocating for me to bring him over to meet mom and dad.

Our parents were very modern for their age. It was the extended family that I was worried about. The bitter aunt who lived to compare her children's successes with those of everyone else, the cousin who somehow seemed to fall for the same guys I did, and the very wealthy uncle who used every family gathering to flaunt his rands... Nairas... new Merc... Rolex watch... and even the new girlfriend that's always younger than the one before.

I was worried that they would not want to look beyond his hazel eyes and brown hair, and they would make it difficult for him to adjust. I was not worried about myself... that Gabe might get to know my family and want to run away as fast as he could.

"I love you, Zee. No matter what." It is in those words that I knew he would stay for a little while longer. Just like that, I was reminded of why I was in love with his beautiful soul.

"I love you more."

"Not possible."

"You saying I'm lying?"

"Yes, because you have no idea what I see in you. If only you had a glimpse... a taste." Oh, God!

"How did I not meet you before?" the words fall from my lips, but it's my heart that wants to know.

"I'm glad I got to meet you at all."

"I am going to cry, Gabe," I warn, unwilling to put on a public spectacle.

"You still look amazing with tears on your face."

"My mother is going to think you did something to me."

"I will explain that it's all you, the doing I mean?"

"You're not asking to be slapped are you?"

"Spanking me in public. Naughty, naughty girl."

"Hahaha, you better be relieved that we're in a public place because if I had to even name one thing I would do to you if we weren't, I would be breaking about fifty laws and I am too sexy to be a felon."

"The idea of an orange jumpsuit on you does turn me on."

"Gabe I am warning you..."

"Tell that to Magic Mike, not me."

"Who in the hell is Magic Mike?" I ask, defeated.

"The other guy… down there… how can you not know who Magic Mike is after all he has done for you?" Gabe replies and winks conspiringly.

"Well because no one calls you… or him… Magic Mike?" I can't help but roll my eyes.

"You did… once… when we did that thing with the chocolate sauce…"

"Gabe!"

"…on the side of the bed… you loved him then."

"Gabe… people are looking at us."

"They always are though. Should we really give them something to look at?"

"No, I mean they are actually *looking* at us. People heard you."

"Don't be shy now, you've done worse."

My sister is waiting for us when we touch down at Oliver Tambo International Airport and I can feel my heart do that thing that it does when someone I love is nearby. I'm happy to be home already. It must have been a while because I can see a little bump underneath her oversized t-shirt. She has dragged her husband out here too.

I cannot imagine him not doing anything for Namhla. She squeals in innocent but captivating delight as we walk out of the luggage area. I can hear Gabe take deep breaths, reassuring himself. I hold his hand to let him know that it doesn't matter what the world thinks of him because I happen to think the world of him.

"Look at you two! Oh my gosh! You look amazing, Sisi!" Namhla comments loudly.

"Thank you, Nam. And you look like someone bathed you in Vaseline."

"Oh, I have so much to tell you. Mom does not even know."

"That you're pregnant? How did you keep that from her third eye?"

"I have been avoiding her. I knew you would know immediately."

"Of course, what are sister radars for? You are glowing! I am so happy for you."

"Thank you."

"And you're not yet fat so that's good to see."

"Don't say it... Sizwe wants a boy."

"Well, I don't care what he wants. I need a girl and you know I'm always right."

We get so lost in our sisterly bonding that I completely forget about Gabe, but Sizwe (not my brother, Sizwe; my sister's husband, who is also Sizwe) hugs him and helps with the bags.

"Don't feel bad? They just need a moment to let it all out. I have been married three years and I can tell you now, it does not get any better."

"I see, they look happy."

"They are happy. Sorry man, I'm Sizwe, Namhla's husband, and I can tell by the look on your face that you thought I was her brother."

"No, you don't look at her like she's your sister. I'm Gabe."

"No, I don't. Welcome to the family, Gabe."

"Thank you."

"Don't be nervous, you will fit right in. As long as you don't confuse anyone with the other, because I am telling you, my man, not all black people look the same."

"I'll remember that."

Standing somewhere in the middle of the airport, a huge sigh leaves Gabe's lips. Love is doing the impossible right now. He would walk through the fire for Zee, what could a mere family gathering do to a lifetime of planned happiness?

CHAPTER 15

Right decisions don't always come from the best intentions

I was filled with an overwhelming desire to see Sabelo after my talk with Sibahle - even if it's from a distance; but how do you see someone when they have Chichi guarding them? I didn't think Sabelo knew how I felt about him; but then again, I didn't even know how I felt about him exactly. He was broody in a way that I found to be very sexy. I heard that he was back from Cape Town, a doctor now, and was working in the Eastern Cape. So I started pestering my mom every chance I got to allow me to go visit my grandparents.

"You cannot just up and leave mid-semester and go to the Eastern Cape, Melisa. Do you think you are the professor wena? That you don't need to study and pass like the other children at your school?"

"Ma, I am already getting distinctions in all my modules. I don't even need to write exams this year."

"Says who? So now you think you are smart."

There was no winning with my mother, but I was a very motivated girl.

"Mom, it's Visual Arts, I'm not running for president, and I'm good at what I do."

"Yoh, lom'twana! See, this is why I told your father that he cannot allow children to do whatever they want. Why did you not go study a BCom or medicine like other children?"

It was a rhetorical question and answering it was asking for the death penalty, but I needed to get away from Bloemfontein as fast as I could and as quickly as possible.

"Because I hate accounting and I fail maths. I'm good at art, Ma."

"And what exactly are you going to do with a BA in Visual arts? Apply to be homeless?"

"That's not fair."

"Is it not? Because I'm not planning on supporting you for the rest of your life, Mel. You are 22 my baby, and I want you to be successful in whatever you do. I want you to get a job that pays well and to work hard and live a good life. Do I need to be fair for that?"

"I guess not… but then it's a good thing my father is white, and I have a trust fund."

To which my mother had no answer or was maybe choosing not to indulge me. My mother and I were different in a way that she had to work hard to be where she was, while I had been born with a silver spoon in my mouth. I had gotten a car at eighteen (which she vehemently denied me using until my 21st birthday) and maybe she thought I would grow up to be entitled. I was anything but entitled. I was very down-to-earth.

In the end, she allowed me to go to the Eastern Cape for a weekend - after I had promised it was to look at the landscape from Gogo Khesiwe's house and gain inspiration.

"Okay, go, but don't you come crying to me when you fail."

"I told you mommy... failing is not in my genes."

The trip to the Eastern Cape was cursed from the get-go. First, the bus was four hours late (much to my mother's delight), and I had to wait at the information center in nothing but a dress and a cardigan, shivering, while my mother called every 10 minutes to rub salt into the open wound.

"Have you left yet?"

"Not since you last called."

"Don't be mad at me baby, you are the one that wanted to go."

"And I will let you know as soon as I leave, Ma."

"Your sister wants to talk to you. I don't understand why she is so excited that you are going to my mother's house. Is there something that I should know, Mel?"

"Did she say anything?"

"Would I be asking if she did?"

"No, but you have nothing to worry about, Ma." A lie.

"You do know that I always find out, right? I hope you don't forget that just because you think you are old enough. I'm still your mother."

I wanted to blurt out that I knew but I was not going to fall for my mother's bait. I knew what she was thinking, and I was not going to give her the satisfaction that she was spot on. I was going to hunt down the guy I like and tell him how I felt even though he was engaged to someone else... and I was going to hold my breath as he told me what I already knew, "I'm sorry that's how you feel, Mel; but I'm with Chichi."

Even at 22, my mother was overprotective when it came to guys. Heck, at my age I'm ancient in the sense that I should not even be a Mary. I should have at least three heartbreaks have had an abortion and have been in a serious relationship with a guy who is not marrying someone else. I understood where she was coming from, though. She had been young and in love when she had met my dad and the fact that they didn't work out must have hurt her a lot, and now she wanted to protect me from the same unfortunate story. Only I felt that I was running out of time. How could I learn if I was too afraid to try?

I asked to talk to Sibahle and assured my mother that I loved her.

"Hi, mtase. Why do I have to hear from mom that you're going to the Eastern Cape?"

"Well, because I knew what you were going to say, and I didn't want a reason not to go."

"Oh my word, are you seriously doing it? Now? Now? I cannot believe it."

"Don't be so loud. Isn't mom with you?"

"Seriously do you think I would be so stupid as to be in the same room with her when you're telling me that you're going to take Chichi's man? Give me some credit. So how are you feeling? Aren't you scared?"

"No, I am fine."

"Liar."

"I don't know what I'm going to do. Or say. I don't even want to think about it. Like what if I say something wrong?" I burst out, without even thinking.

"Oh gosh, you finally sound like a girl. Just breathe, you'll know what to do when you see him, and if you don't then just kiss him," Sibahle replies.

"I wonder how you know so much when you're only thirteen."

"Fourteen, please. I'll be fourteen in three days, and I have the internet for research."

"Okay, I'll tell you everything when I get back."

"No, no, no… you are texting me every step of the way. What if Chichi scratches your face and no one knows where you are?"

"Seriously Sibahle, I won't die from a scratch."

"It's Chichi we're talking about, don't forget that. She'll do worse if she finds out you're after her man. And you are white, and might just bleed to death."

"Okay, you are talking fertilizer right now. I'm hanging up. Bye-bye," but I still manage to laugh raucously. Trust my fourteen-year-old baby sister to make me feel good about going after another girl's man while at the same time making me feel bad for being white.

I close my ears and try to picture Sabelo. I wonder if he is still sullen and walking like he just doesn't want to. He will tell me how he loves my smile and reminds me of how I always look down when I'm feeling overwhelmed. I was 13 then and he was four years older, but he was everything I had dreamed of in a guy. I smile and wonder if I should tell him that I never told my grandmother that he was the one who used to steal her chickens and if he will realize that it is because I like him.

I try to picture him with a beard, and muscles all over his body, wearing a white coat over and a stethoscope around his neck, listening to my heartbeat. Then I'm drawn back to the present by a weird feeling and thoughts of how what I am planning to do is in no way morally right, even though it is with the very best of intentions. How would I feel if I was in Chichi's shoes (although those would be very high-heeled shoes)? How would I feel if the man I was going to marry was being hunted by another woman?

Disregarding the undeniable fact that my mother raised me well (bless her soul), I argue with my conscience about being in love with the very same guy who is set to marry the queen. Yet, what good is being morally correct if I lose out on my happily ever after? Sometimes a girl has to do what a girl has to do.

CHAPTER 16

Pride... The burden of a foolish man

The radio show was going well, and (despite the emotional challenges we've had of late) Tuks and I were in a good place. We were not talking as much as we were before, but that can be blamed on my busy schedule and his scrambling to pass and graduate. I desperately needed to believe that we were okay.

I liked spending time with him and having the freedom to return to my life and be free of commitments at the same time. Not having to care too much about anyone and dancing to the beat of my drum.

"I haven't seen you in a while," I say slowly as I put on my clothes.

"I've been busy, and so have you." He replies half-heartedly and doesn't look at me.

"That's true... but I haven't even been seeing you around on campus, which is weird."

"It is?" This is a question alright, but there is something in the air afterward.

"Yeah."

"Well, I can't apologize for not being around whenever you want to fuck." The words fall hard and fast as bullets shot from a rifle.

"Okay, okay… wait a minute. I'm not complaining. I just…"

"You miss me… dammit you won't die if you say it, Moon."

"You know I don't like all of that. I like what we have."

"I know you do." And even though I believe he is being honest, the way he says it still feels peculiar to me.

"Look, I know I can't read people, Tokgamo, but the truth is that you are different; and I don't just mean in bed."

"Is that a good or a bad thing?"

"Hahaha, I wouldn't be coming back if it was bad. It's just different." This part is true.

Then he kisses me, sensually this time and with more intent that for a second I forget my not staying over rule. I like how his lips seem to know exactly where to go and what to do with mine. If this does not deserve to get the best friends-with-benefits-of-the-year award then I don't know what does.

I close my eyes and let his tongue work its miracles while he unbuttons my shirt. He bites my lips, and every part of my body goes insane. Digging my nails into his back I breathe heavily, and he lets out a groan. We've fucked before, and it has always been perfect, but there's something about what he is doing to my sanity and self-control right now that makes me think of a song by Alex and Sierra. "Oh, this is where it starts tonight. If you open up your heart tonight."

There is something in those words that frightens me more than death. I don't even like indie music but somehow spending time with Tuks has me listening to what he listens to even when he is not around. The way he is acting can only mean that he's changed somehow and things are bound to change. I don't like change.

He keeps biting my ear and drawing circles on my chest and although he's done this often, it feels very different this time. When we are done and are all sweaty, and for the first time I'm not rushing to take a shower to erase the warmth he has left on my body, he looks at me and gets up from the bed.

"That, Moon, is how normal people make love."

I put my clothes on and it seems like I have lost all knowledge of what I'm doing. We don't say anything after these words, and I have to run from his place right after. My head is not spinning, it rather feels like he has kissed away every trace of logic from my head. I'm just numb.

I sprint to my place, relieved that Zee is away for the long weekend. I desperately need this time alone but need to talk to someone… to my mother, but I haven't spoken to her in a while and I'm not in a forgiving mood. So, I go through my contacts and see Samora's number. He is a guy I met in my first year who is smart, gorgeous, and talented. We had a thing, and it was good, but if I had to compare, Tuks ranks way higher. Also, he had a girlfriend last time I checked but who cares? I send him a text and wait patiently. My phone rings in less than five minutes and I jump at the unfamiliar sound that breaks my moment of solitude.

"Hello."

"Hey, stranger. This is a surprise."

"I know. I didn't think you were still alive."

"You are the one that walked away, remember?"

"And you are the one that didn't stop me, remember?"

He laughs. "You're still witty I see, I guess that means that nothing has changed."

"I don't know, do you want anything to change?"

"With you? No way..."

"I'll see you in fifteen."

"See you in fifteen."

Samora doesn't tell me about his girlfriend, and I don't ask. I don't want to know, because right now I just want to not have to think about anything. My mother is disappointed in me because I refuse to accept or even meet the supposed brother that I have, and now I have to deal with Tuks summoning feelings that I did not know I even possessed.

I don't like that my whole life is falling apart right in front of my eyes, and there is nothing that I can do to make it okay. I have always been in control and this feeling of helplessness makes me have trust issues. I cannot just sit and watch everything go to the dogs, and allow a nobody to claim my father and destroy every sense of respect I had for him. I am my father's daughter after all.

"Hello UCT and our listeners from around Cape Town. I'm Moon Mosiapoa and this is the evening show, Politricks. Welcome aboard. Before we get on with the tricks and nuances of the political world I am going to start our journey with a song by Cyndi Lauper, "Girls just want to have fun". This feel-good song is a go-to song for my inner feminist alter ego and should be an anthem for every girl child, and woman out there. Enjoy."

I come home in the morning light
My mother says when you gonna live your life right
Oh mother dear we're not the fortunate ones
And girls they want to have fun
Oh girls just want to have fun

The phone rings in the middle of the night
My father yells what you gonna do with your life
Oh daddy dear you know you're still number one
But girls they want to have fun
Oh girls just want to have fun

Some boys take a beautiful girl
And hide her away from the rest of the world
I want to be the one to walk in the sun
Oh girls they want to have fun
Oh girls just want to have

"Welcome back again. If you've just joined us I'm Moon Mosiapoa and that was an eighties classic by, the ever-so-talented, Cyndi Lauper. The woman ages like wine. Looking gorgeous for her age. Talking about wine… well, alcohol in this case, the story of the girl who was gang raped after having her drink spiked at a party is still making headlines. It has been two weeks and somehow the University has not succeeded in getting the boys who did this apprehended.

After years of having women get the same opportunities as men, you would expect the people who our parents entrust to be responsible for our safety when we are at school to at the very least give up the names of these suspects. As a female and a student at this university, you have to wonder if the reason the authorities are dragging their feet is that the victim is female, or if it is because she is black.

Maybe if we explore the racial propaganda our voices will be heard, because her plight as a female has unfortunately fallen on deaf ears. No one cares if it's a gender issue, but people start to worry when we start talking about race. I need to feel safe, and I can only get to that point when I know that the law is on my side.

My producer has just alerted me that there is an incoming caller. "Hello anonymous caller, welcome to Politricks, where all the dirty laundry is aired."

"Good show," Rory comments as I walk out of the booth. He is the producer. I smile and walk to where I must have left my cell phone and handbag and maybe even next week's preparation notes. I hope to find them under the pile of papers on my desk. I really need to start being more organized and get rid of the mumbo jumbo that I, unfortunately, find comfort in, because it has gotten so serious that sometimes I end up finding important work only after months of searching.

"Thank you," I reply as I pass him, but he has the menacing look of pure obliteration in his eyes, like a cat that just caught the biggest rat alive.

"What is it, Rory? I know you and that sly look is not because we are a step closer to solving this case. So spare me the drama and talk."

I hope it is something I can handle right now because I have been feeling some type of way for the past few days, and what's hard is that my lack of patience has a lot to do with how I've been feeling about the way things ended... or sort of ended with

Tuks because we didn't talk about it… and less to do with the fact that Samora has been filling in most of the blanks.

"A girl is waiting for you outside."

"A girl?" I ask, confused because I don't have a lot of female friends. Maybe he meant to say Zimkhita, but she is home introducing Gabe to her parents for the first time.

"Yes, a girl, and she is mad. So mad I had to offer her some of my ADD pills." Rory answers dramatically followed by another theatrical gesture.

I shake my head, sit down on the nearest chair, and start rocking. My feet hurt, my head hurts from overthinking the fight with my mother, and for no apparent reason I've been missing Motswedi a lot lately. Having to stare at Rory's smug face does nothing for my determination to push everything to the back of my head and sleep like a baby tonight.

I take my right hand and unconsciously rub it against the scar on my left hand and this time I do not stop. It has been a while since I thought about him, and I hate to admit that I miss him so much it hurts.

"So why is she mad?" I ask trying to deflect the train of thoughts that clouds my mind.

"I don't know. Are you not going to go outside and see who she is or what she wants? I told her you would be out in five minutes and that was 10 minutes ago."

"Why were you so forthcoming?" I tease, and kick him playfully "Did she show you her boobs?"

"No, but she's with a guy, and he looks very familiar." He comments and kicks me back, but the words make everything go in slow motion for a while.

"Who is it?" I ask cautiously, trying to simmer the curiosity burning on my tongue, and stand up. I stop rubbing my arm till the next time I need a pick-me-up, but Rory shakes his head and walks away without saying another word. I click my tongue, kick off my shoes and run outside to find Samora standing with his back towards me and his head leaning inwards. I smile ruefully. We were not scheduled to meet tonight but he came, nonetheless.

I'm still smiling as I walk towards him until I catch an image of what fits the description of the girl who's been looking for me. I think the angry girl may be his girlfriend.

"Is this her?" she hisses, and he nods quickly, which only adds to my confusion. She screamed loud and murderously before I can ask what is going on, "You bitch!" Then she slaps me hard across the face. My hand instinctively flies to cover my face, but I do not hear anything else because of the ringing in my ears. I want to slap her back, as I should, but every sense in my body has gone numb. The embarrassing reality hits me… I just got slapped by a girl. Someone's girlfriend for that matter.

CHAPTER 17

And when you fall, fall hard

"Oh my gosh! What have you been eating though, Nam-Nam? Like is this a weird pregnancy thing or have you always just liked food?" I tease my sister about her weight gain and she attempts to slap me, but I duck and hide behind Gabe.

We are at my parents' house, and it's been a very busy day. Everyone wants to know who this white boy is and what he is doing in Roodepoort. My sister and her husband have done everything possible to make him feel welcome, and my parents have not been too bad either. It's my brothers that I'm not so sure about, and since we've been here three days and they still haven't arrived, I'm still holding out a prayer.

"Look at you two. You are just too adorable."

"I told you he was hot."

"He is. Good choice, Sissy."

And once again Gabe is subjected to having my sister and I talk about him as if he is not here. He smiles, he's is used to it and knowing my baby, he does not mind at all, and is just happy to see me happy.

"Well, what can I say? I wouldn't necessarily choose a scarecrow and spend the rest of my life as Beauty living with the Beast."

"With you as the Beast, of course," Gabe interjects and I jab him with my finger.

"Oh, I see we're getting comfortable at Zee's house now aren't we? The airport is just an hour away."

"I love you too."

"My gosh! You two make me want to cry. This is beautiful."

"Thank you, ma'am."

"Ma'am? Excuse me how old do you think I am Gabe?"

"Young enough."

"Good save. Namhla was going to have you as one of her cravings."

"Yes. Hahaha, don't refer to me like you would your boring history teacher from high school, just call me Namhla. We're practically family now."

"Okay, can someone put on the brakes here? Why are you fawning over him? First, mom made him tea in the morning, and dad sat for an hour with him last night talking about rugby. When did dad start watching rugby? And now you."

"Dad has been watching rugby with me." Sizwe chirps in and I understand. Sizwe is one of those hot-blooded Zulu men who grew up in Kwa-Zulu Natal and went to those all-boys private schools which saw him play rugby for the best part of his life, and now he is changing the best part about uBaba. My dad used to love watching soccer with me.

"Don't mind her, "Namhla whispers to Gabe, ignoring the fact that I can hear them. "She has always loved the attention."

I take a moment to look around and I can't help but smile. My mother is with my aunt deciding on what dressing to put in the salad. My father is barking orders at my third cousin, Jali (who just got released from jail) to set up the tables and chairs in the tent. My younger cousins are huddled in a corner gossiping about who kissed who on *Skeem Saam* and who broke up with who on *Big Brother*. I see my gorgeous sister, the ever-jovial and genuine Namhla, and I can't help but feel like I'm on top of the world. I love my family, and it has been both scary and interesting to see how they interact with Gabe. With his charming features and enticing smile, he has had no problem fitting in.

"Your family is amazing."

"Gabe, they are loud... and this is not even everyone. My gangster uncle still has to come by in his latest Merc or whatever sports car he is rolling around with these days. That man is a show-off, so just compliment him on everything and don't stare at his girlfriend. My brother got into trouble because he was flirting with the latest girlfriend the other time."

Gabe just laughs at this. It's as if he has spent his whole life around these crazy people and its all normal for him.

"Oh, and aunt Zanele will be here too. She's my favorite, even though I try not to show it. She's the sweetest."

"I wish I had this."

"What? A drunk uncle who fondles you at a family gathering?"

"No, family. This whole atmosphere... I grew up alone and my parents are at least a hundred years older than me. So I never knew what it felt like to have people around you who were entirely different from you, but you could still get along and have fun."

"If you call Jali asking Sizwe for money every five seconds fun then by all means let's switch. "

That conversation made me realize just how different Gabe and I are. A simple Sunday lunch at my mother's house includes both my parents, my sister, her husband, my older brother (bhut'Sizwe) his wife, their son, my eldest brother (bhut'Mthunzi), his wife, and their twin daughters… and that's not even a family gathering. When we really get together it includes everyone from Natal, Mpumalanga, Lesotho, and Johannesburg is called upon.

Gabe grew up not having to share anything with anyone, whilst I had to fight for everything from my mother's peanut butter biscuits to the chocolates that my father bought for us when he came home from work at the month's end. I had to learn how to stand up for myself by the time I was five because bhut'Sizwe used to beat up the children ekasi so they would pick up on me when he wasn't around. Yet, despite being at odds with Namhla about *everything*, I can't imagine not having her around to teach me how to apply makeup, or telling me to get myself together after crying myself into a stupor because a boy had broken my heart.

"Do you think your family likes me?"

"Likes you? Huh, that's an understatement. Apart from my cousin Loyiso giving you the side eye because his perverted self thinks he and I are meant to be together. They love you."

"So I fit right in?"

"Like you are the bastard child. Hahaha, it's nauseating actually."

"Don't be jealous."

"Me, jealous of you? Please!"

"My parents haven't met you but already they admire you."

"How could they not? I'm amazing."

"Modest much?"

"You made me into a narcissist, you know that? You are always saying the right things. I love you."

"I really cannot imagine spending the rest of my life with anyone but you."

Then Namhla calls to tell us that people have arrived and we should change. It's a formal event, and my inner diva self-high fives herself. I'm wearing a striped navy crop top, a cream-white flair skirt, and some killer stilettos. Gabe is wearing a navy-blue blazer, tight cream pants that match my skirt, and a black t-shirt. Narcissist or not, we sure do look good.

"I have a surprise for you," I say, as we leave the room to go to the tent outside.

"Unless you are telling me that I'm amazing I don't want to hear."

"Depends on how you want to take it... or should I say it to Magic Mike."

This stops him in his tracks, as I expected, and it makes me laugh out loud. The look on his face is priceless.

"I am listening."

"You or Magic Mike?"

"Both of us."

I want to leave him hanging but the sad look on his face tugs at my heart. "I am wearing silk panties."

"Damn Zee, your family is here."

"I know, I just want you to think about how you are taking them off later tonight."

"With my teeth of course," Gabe promises, and the sound of his ragged breath against my skin makes me shiver in expectant delight. This is going to be one long event… celebrating thirty long years.

CHAPTER 18

Even your favorites don't make it to the end

From the moment I arrive at my grandmother's house, tired, hungry, and heavy-laden with a weekend bag, she is all over me like a rash. I wonder if there is something that my mother told her that I don't know. Usually, uGog'Khesiwe is happier to see Mxolisi and she is nonchalant towards me and Sibahle, but today she is grinning wider than usual, her love over pouring.

"How was the trip? Your mother told me that the bus was late. Shame poor thing, you had to wait in that cold place all that time. Come let me make you coffee."

"It was okay, Gogo. You know these busses, but I'm here now."

"I cooked your favourite. Samp and beans. You can eat after taking a bath... get rid of those evil spirits that followed you from the big city."

"Gogo, I will eat and bathe later. I only have today to work on my art and I cannot miss the sunset."

"Yintoni le art yakho? Why can't you be a doctor like lomfana, uSabelo?"

"Because I am not good at maths and physics like uSabelo, Gogo, and I cannot stand blood or sores. Oh no, thank you!"

"Ya, idemocracy that is doing this."

I hate having to lie to my grandmother, but I have only a few hours to finally do what has kept me awake for about a month, so I quickly brush my teeth, wash my face, and change into a long tight black dress that compliments my figure and complexion.

"So you have to brush your teeth for iart yakho?"

"Gogo, I spent twelve hours on the road. I have to look like I come from the big city and not from a mine."

"For who?" she asks suspiciously, not buying my story one bit.

"No one. I will see you later tonight." I reply before dashing out of the house.

It's the last house behind the mountain, and the first next to the river, so I have to walk around the river bend before I can see the main road leading to Sabelo's house. I look back and see my grandmother watching me and I contemplate taking the long route as if I am going to the shops, but then I feel like shouting "Screw it!" I walk on, positive that she is watching my every move.

Life in the village is so that everyone knows everyone else's business, and it doesn't surprise me that people are already coming out of their houses to watch me. You can count on the fact that before the sun goes down everyone will be talking about how the white girl from Khesiwe's house went to see the doctor boy who is set to marry another girl. My art bag already feels heavy by the time I make it around the river, and my arm hurts like crazy. Funny thing is that art is the last thing on my mind at this very moment.

I see the Dlodlo house, painted bright pink with very big windows and I spot the tree we used to play under as kids. I think that's the same tree Sabelo broke his arm from climbing up top to retrieve a ball someone had kicked into the branches, but I'd have to take a closer look to be sure.

The closer I get the tenser I become. There's an uncomfortable taste in my mouth, something like bile. I have never puked from anxiety so maybe this is my first. I get to the gate and take a deep breath. No one is outside but the windows and doors are open, so hopefully, someone is home. At this point my feet feel like lead, and it's taking every bit of my will to not turn right back and go home to the comfort of my grandmother's warm meal and freshly brewed coffee. I see a shadow behind the house, and call out to it.

"Hello."

It is silent for a while, and I wonder if I should have called out in isiXhosa instead. People in rural areas tend to be very protective of their language, but before I can mutter a "molweni", he comes towards me with an axe in one hand and sweat dripping from his face. He's not wearing a tee shirt, and I have to bite my tongue to stop myself from drooling.

"Hello yourself." His voice sounds like the type of voice you'd hear on the radio. It's become gruff with age and the way the words fall so easily out of his mouth makes me wonder if I am doing the right thing. I attempt to laugh as I take in his features. He is tall, very tall, in fact, taller than the last time I saw him, but this is understandable because it's been nine years.

"Hey," I say again unable to gather the right words. He is still staring at me, taking me in and I have to thank Legit for making figure-hugging black dresses.

"Hey," he says again, and continues to stare, his eyes challenging me to say something.

We are both silent for a while, and it seems like time has stood still. I'm getting nervous now and it is at this exact moment that I wish I had my blog to do the talking for me. I am not good at face-to-face confrontations because I get anxious, but I'm great at hiding behind the computer while speaking my mind.

Sabelo has changed a lot, but at the same, time he hasn't changed a bit. To me, he is still the same boy who used to run around with his friends playing marbles and kicking sand. The same boy one who never made me feel different for looking like a white kid when everyone else teased me for my shameful attempt at a legit Xhosa accent. That very one who used to steal my grandmother's chickens and I've liked from a very long time ago… he just happens to be somebody else's future husband.

"You always were shy weren't you?" he breaks the silence and I want to hug him. I smile shyly and fiddle with my art bag which I have forgotten was heavy.

"Yes. Uhm…"

"My parents are not home if that's who you were looking for."

"Parents, no. I was actually looking for you."

"Me? This must be good. I thought you had forgotten about me."

"No."

"It's been nine years."

"I know. Not that I was counting or anything."

“I was.” He says softly, and I forget to breathe. Then as if the moment has not passed between us, he gestures to my satchel and a wicked grin passes over his face.

“You still draw, don’t you? I still have the first picture you ever gave me.”

“What!?” I do not even remember what picture he is talking about but the artist in me is deeply intrigued. “I have drawn so many things I cannot even remember what I’ve done or haven’t.”

“As I said, I’ve been counting. It was a very long time ago. You were still in braids and braces, and it was of that very tree.” Then he points to the tree that he fell from attempting to play Robin Hood. I laugh because it’s true what they say, you never forget your first.

“Oh, my word yes. I remember you took it from me. I didn’t give it to you.”

“You were going to. You just didn’t know it yet.” He says with such intensity that I wonder if he is talking about my heart or my art. “So I guess you are here to retrace your steps? Draw the same tree I mean?”

“No actually… I came because… I mean, it’s been a while since I last saw you…and yes… that tree has always been my inspiration… but… you are getting married.”

“Are you asking or telling me?” he responds, and time stops.

“I heard people talk and it’s good,” I reply, although my heart wants to walk out of my chest and slap some reality into me, my mouth is the one to do it. I blurt out before I can stop myself, “and I’ve always liked you.”

It is only when he drops the axe and becomes silent that I realize that maybe, just maybe we are not meant to figure it all out when we are young and naïve… when life is all peaches and roses in our twenties. That perhaps we are supposed to embarrass ourselves, make mistakes, and say things without thinking, knowing full well that the consequence is that we are going to spend the whole night regretting everything and nursing a glass of tequila. Maybe, just maybe, life doesn't just give you lemons, it happens to throw you a rope, but it's up to you how you are going to pull yourself out of the hole.

"Why did you wait so long?" he asks, and I can hear the accusation in his voice.

"Because I'm Melisa. I'm shy and I love to draw things and I write blogs. I don't always know what to do, and I am so sorry for blurting this to you because you have someone. I was not thinking. I've wanted to do this for a long time but was scared, but then I started walking and kept walking, and before I knew it I was on your doorstep calling out... I'm talking too much, aren't I?"

"No, you're saying everything that I should have said a very long time ago."

The last thing I remember is that his hands were holding my face and he was staring into my eyes so hard that I started crying. Maybe our saving grace is to trust ourselves enough to do the wrong thing for the right reason.

CHAPTER 19

Mothers and Daughters

My mother has flown all the way to Cape Town to tell me that we have to talk. I have been ignoring her calls, texts, and emails ever since that day at the restaurant. The truth is that I don't want her to have to feel the obligation to explain anything to me because that will mean she will have to tell me the truth, and I do not think that I'm ready for that yet.

She is standing in the middle of my dormitory, regal sand unflinching. She could be doing something as unimportant as reading a recipe and it would still sound grand. I have to admit that even though I haven't seen her in months, she is still very beautiful. She has box braids on and fiery red lipstick, a white Versace trench coat, and gorgeous Aldo heels that I'd like to take off her hands.

"I do not care what you have to say, but Moon you need to grow up."

"Of course, you don't care, because if you did you would've heard me loud and clear. I don't want to talk about anything, and I'm not meeting any half-brother, this doppelganger you have unearthed from the pits of wherever."

"Moon Mosiapoa do not dare..."

"Mama what am I supposed to say? That I'm happy that I have a brother from God-knows-where?"

"You have to accept it. You think you're the only one shocked about this?" she asks with regret on her tongue, and looks at me quizzically.

"Well you seem to be dealing very well with the news, you even bought the latest Aldo heels." They are part of the current autumn collection.

"Don't be ridiculous Moon, this has nothing to do with my shoes."

"But it has something to do with your money, right? It's always about the money, Ma."

"If that's how you live your life then I have to admit that I've failed at doing a good job raising you."

"Mom, I grew up richer than most people. My father was a powerful man, and my mother was on the cover of magazines from the time she was 17. I learned how to spot people who just wanted to be close to me because of what I had from a young age. I know when people want my money. How come you don't?"

"The world is not in black and white, Moon. Your father was powerful, yes, but he had a life before you, and maybe you don't want to hear it but sometimes when the truth is staring you in the face you have to accept it."

"But he would have told me if I had a brother, Ma. He would have."

"He didn't even tell me, baby. I don't even think he knew."

"Then how did *he* find out?"

"From his mother's diary."

"A diary, Ma. Seriously? You humor me. How authentic can that thing be?"

"Something tells me that he's not lying. You can't lie about things like this without being able to keep it up."

"It's called being a pathological liar."

"Can you at least meet him and see who he is, and what he wants? He is a nice person, baby."

"No."

"Moon..."

"No, Ma, what for? Talk about *my* father over coffee and jam tarts?"

"For goodness sake, you are overdoing this whole my-father-was-a-hero thing. Bakang was the best thing to ever happen to me, I loved that man and I still do five years after he passed. I can't help but search for his eyes in the people that I meet. So don't act like you are the only one that lost something, because I lost everything. So you are going to meet your brother and you are going to laugh and pretend to be happy about it... because no matter what you think... you can't live your life trying to live up to your father's image."

I do not hear the next words because there is a sound coming from the room that sounds like a lost puppy, and it takes me a while to realize that it is coming from me. I haven't cried in years... and it takes both my mother and me by surprise. I sit on the bed and bite my lips hard to keep from being overheard. My mother instinctively reaches for me and the warmth I feel from her arms is both soothing and scary. When did I become this person? When did I become so cold that any sort of attachment makes me run for the hills?

"It's okay. It's okay to let it out."

"I can't..."

"Yes, you can."

"No, I can't, Ma... I am not ready just yet."

"It's okay. Take all the time you need."

I did not mean to cry, I really didn't, but after years of trying hard to build the perfect image, it became easy to kick everything down. People do not know this but there's a lot of pressure when you are the daughter of really famous people. People expect you to talk a certain way, to walk a certain way, and they watch you when you're eating when you're laughing, and they wait very patiently for that moment when you just miss one step to pounce and celebrate.

So I worked extra hard to prove them wrong from early on until I did not know what failure was. While my friends were smoking weed I was involved with charities that were dedicated to supporting cancer patients. While my friends were getting drunk at Club Moffet, I was pulling all-nighters studying for exams so I could keep that perfect grade and when my friends fell in love I chose to be smart and I told myself that love was just a distraction.

I did all of this because I did not want to end up on the front cover of Shwashwi as the life of a party in Hillbrow, or as the other woman in a messy relationship. People respected my father and regarded him as a hero... and I wanted to be just like him... the hero's daughter.

"You have to go now. I have a radio show to prepare for."

"Baby, all work and no play made Jane the boring girl next door."

"Says the woman who has been working since she was 17."

"It was different for me. I was a model and I still made time to be like the other normal children my age."

"Well, dad always told me that perseverance meant stopping, not because you are tired but because the task is done."

"Your father was a very smart man, but baby it's a Friday night. Don't you have friends that at least go out to clubs?"

"Not really. Zee went home, and I don't really do the whole friendship thing. People lie and I cannot deal with any of that."

My mother sighs in exasperation and she flings her hands in the air. "Tell me I am not to blame for this. Tell me this is all Pricilla's doing."

"Oh, she made my life miserable."

"She did as best as anyone could," and despite her greatest efforts my mother can't help but laugh.

"She made me drink milk every night. I swear that's the reason why I'm lactose intolerant."

"There were times I wanted to save you, shame nana."

"Why didn't you?"

"Because I knew you would be fine... Besides, you've always been your father's daughter."

A moment passes between us, and we are both silent. "Alzheimer's sucks, doesn't it?" I finally ask my mom and she replies.

"It sucks ass." It is the first time I hear her swear at something other than a taxi driver and I cannot help but laugh. "Don't you ever repeat that!"

"No ma'am. I can't have Pricilla washing my mouth with soap. Do you think he's proud of me?" I ask quietly, wondering if I turned out okay. Mom stares at me for a second before kissing me on the forehead (something my father used to do).

"Always. You aren't on drugs and haven't needed rehab, so he is extremely proud of you."

I don't say this out loud, but I hope that she is right. No drugs yes, no rehab for her alcohol-addicted daughter either but I could do with a time out from sleeping around and getting slapped by angry girlfriends. When did I become this?

"How are you doing?" she then asks after what seems like an eternity. "I mean, really doing?"

A part of me wants to keep my defenses up and say that I'm doing well, that I'm okay. I know she's not asking about my health, or whether I have a boyfriend that she can at least be hopeful about someday turning into a son-in-law. She is asking about that night, two years back when I first got the scar on my hand.

"I don't know. I don't think about it as much as I used to."

"Is that a good thing?"

"I don't know either because I am afraid to forget about him."

"I know honey."

"I am afraid to forget about both of them. It's as if I'm forever living my life to make them proud of me and me… I get really…

I do not want to fail, Ma." I am breaking down for the second time, something I have not done so well in a while.

"Hush now baby. It is going to be okay. Mommy is here."

I got the scar on my left hand from a clean gunshot wound. The shooter, a man who was never caught, missed me but somehow managed to pump six bullets into my best friend's body. I gained a scar that night and lost my bank of emotions. I learned, as Motswedi's body lay lifeless in my arms and I kept screaming for him to wake up, that sometimes the pain of losing someone you care about is greater than having cared for that person.

The scar, a result of my timeous grief, is a constant reminder that everyone I get close to somehow manages to leave me. First, my father, who even from the grave still manages to push me to wake up every morning and try to make him proud. Then Motswedi, who (despite being addicted to Maryjane and light-skinned girls with pretty eyes, even after I punched him in preschool for being a douche) was the salt to my pepper and I trusted him more than the tea in my sugar.

So yes, it does not take a genius to figure out that I'm unable to care about people because when they leave they take a part of you that you can never get back. "He was my best friend, and someone took him away from me."

"I know baby. I know you loved him."

And with this I subconsciously use my right hand, again, to slowly rub the scar on my left hand as if I am somehow bringing him closer to me. I can again feel his warm blood - lots and lots of it - on my body as he took his last breath, and can see his eyes roll back and stop moving as his life ended.

He let a damn bullet get between us. I am mad… raving at myself, at everyone I lost, at everyone who didn't try enough, at the one guy who did try. Everyone knows that even the strongest and smartest girls have a breaking point and once in a while it is right to learn to forgive ourselves or at least live with the promise of forgiveness.

CHAPTER 20

Having not yet learned to let go of old lovers

I am woken by the commotion made by people shouting outside my door. I groan in despair at this downside to being at home with family. Apart from people misusing toilet paper and wearing your clothes, they seem to wake up way before the cock has crowed. It's seven in the morning and I don't think anyone should be allowed to be awake at this time.

I hear my cousin Litha, and then my sister in her screeching voice, attempt to whisper outside of my door, but before I can cry out in despair they open the door. Namhla is the first to come through the door.

"Oh, Sisi, are you okay?"

"No, you just woke me up from a very good dream. What's going on?"

"Oh, you haven't heard?" Litha ventures unceremoniously.

"Heard what Litha? Wait, where is Gabe? Is he okay?" I ask as I jump out of bed and run towards the door. Gabe is not a morning person but somehow he managed to wake up before me and to think that he wasn't even the first thing that came to my mind scares me. Both my sister and cousin are silent, and this does me no good. I hate surprises because I have never been good at receiving them.

"Okay, what is going on? Somebody tell me."

"I am sorry, Sisi."

"It's Kwanele, he was in a car accident this morning and is in a coma."

"I am so sorry, Sisi," Namhla says again but her voice sounds very far away. She tries to hold me, but I pull back. A million things are going through my mind right now and I don't know what to listen to.

"What! How?"

Litha is about to tell me when Namhla stops her. I hear the door open, but I am frozen on the spot and cannot look up and see who it is.

"I can come back later."

"No, it's okay, Gabe. She'll be okay," but the statement only brings worry to his face.

"What happened? Hey, babe... Zee? Baby? Talk to me. What happened to her?" the agony in his voice is unmistakable.

A sharp pain shoots through my heart and I realize this is a feeling from a long time ago that I was once all too familiar with and had hoped that I would never have to feel again. How caustic is it that the very same person who introduced me to this helplessness is doing it again, disputing the fact that it had taken me months to build the shell I hid under till I finally regained the essence I needed to stop crying myself to sleep? It's like I was the one that had lost the foresight to say "Hey sorry, but I'm fucking your best friend." Everyone is talking around me, but I cannot hear them.

"Where is he?" I demand from my sister amid the apocalypse. Namhla gives me an empathetic look and signals me to get up from the bed.

"Milpark Hospital. Are you sure? You don't have to, Sisi. I can get Mihlali to tell us if anything happens," she replies; but it's the way she says that name that makes my heart throb to a sequenced rhythm of numbness.

"No, I want to see him. I want to make sure that she is also holding up okay," I offer. I don't need to explain myself to my sister. She is the one person who understands the depth of this wound because she was there. She was always there.

"Hey, can someone tell me what is going on?" Gabe probes, and just like that I'm thrown back into the present where his appealing smile still manages successfully to dull out any confusion. "Zimkhita, I don't understand what's going on."

My heart sways inconsistently between conflicting feelings of loyalty and honesty. Loyalty to the one I loved before and honesty to the one I'm with now. It is the conclusive factor in every relationship when you have to choose between your past and the promises of a sun-kissed future... when you have to decide whether you want a love that tastes like coffee in the morning all warm and fuzzy or whether you want a love that tastes like whiskey and burns you through your tongue like kerosene. All beautiful and tragic.

I can hear my sister's voice in my head saying "Don't become that girl who wears emptiness like a crown. It becomes too heavy," all too harshly."

"I..." I stop because he won't understand when I say that I chose coffee... that I had always chosen coffee.

"Gabe, I'm sorry," Namhla exclaims, her eyes sloping with shame. "She has to do this."

Litha is the one who butts in and saves me. "We need to leave now if we want to beat the morning traffic."

"I'm coming with," Gabe says to no one in particular, and no one argues with his sense of gallantry, even though it's unusual for a guy to follow his girlfriend to the hospital to go see the ex who left her in a sea of tears.

The drive to the hospital is tense and I can hear the questions that no one wants to ask. I'm echoing them myself, but I also cannot fathom a comprehensible answer. Why am I rushing to see the guy who broke my heart when he left me for my best friend when I should be preparing to go back to the love nest I have built with the one who loves the parts of me that have not yet found their way into a poem? The one who doesn't love me in fragments... who isn't selfish, unsure, and mediocre.

When I see her I am still wrestling with what my heart knows to be right but what my mind believes to be stupid. She is still beautiful but her sunken face brings me no joy. I can't remember a time when she was not happy or smiling when I stalked her. Her smile... her walk... I recognized it in my sleep. I had been so obsessed with trying to figure out why he had chosen her over me that I had found myself living in her shadow.

She looks up and sees me and I notice a light, it flashed through her eye so fast that I don't think it was meant to be there.

"Zimkhita," she calls out my name, but it sounds foreign.

"How is he? Is he okay?" I want to hold her in my arms and hug her so hard it chokes her, but I'm not sure if I'm the right person for that right now. Shaking her head, she responds, but I can see how hard she's trying not to fall apart in front of me.

"Stable but unresponsive. The doctors said that he's stable but unresponsive."

"I'm sorry," I say reassuringly, and I mean it. "I'm so sorry."

"Thank you," Mihlali remarks and continues biting her lower lip until it bruises - a habit of nervousness she has not lost. I know so much about her that it hurts. Once my best friend, she is today a timid woman who is about to lose the father of her son and someone she loves. I am probably the last person she expected to see here reassuring her and trying to ease her pain.

"Can I see him?" I know she might say no because she is uncertain of what I might do, but I'm hoping she sees past the fact that I once hated her with every bone in my body, and understands that we are just two women who love the same man. One right now, the other a very long time ago.

"Yes… he's in there… and..."

"I just want to see him."

"He is not as charming as he once was, but I think he would love to know you were here."

"I hope so," then I turn to Gabe who has been silent this whole time, and grab his hand. "Can you please come with me?" I am not expecting him to say yes but I know that he will do it just for me. He would walk through the fire for me if I asked him to and right now, I want us to both do that. I chose coffee, always.

"Yes."

Despite Gabe's reassuring hand and Mihlali hovering over him, I am still not prepared for what I see. He is as I remember but right now he looks as though he could be somewhere else. He is lying motionless with so many tubes coming out of his body that it is hard to believe he is even human. Mihlali clutches his hand protectively and a tear escapes her almost-dead eyes. She looks like a ghost and I'm once again tempted to reach out and hug her fiercely until life is breathed into her bones.

"It doesn't even look like him. It's like he's already in another world and his body is just here to torture me and remind me that he's not mine." The last four words cause me to look up at her more quickly than I was planning to. I realize the silence in the room is not because Kwanele could die at any second right now but because she is triggering me to say something that I should have said all those years back…"Yes, he was not yours, but you took him anyway."

Regardless of the turn of events, I don't want her to go through what I went through. I don't want her to cry like I did because not everyone can come back from the dead and still live. "He is still here," I say as honestly as possible, "and he is still yours." Talk about being the better person. Maybe forgiveness is not just for the people who have wronged us but, maybe forgiveness is for ourselves too.

We are back in Cape Town and the weather is both cold and unwelcoming, but I love it. I love waking up to a view of the city, and I love how the sea smells in the morning, even from afar. I love opening my eyes to see Gabe in the morning most of all.

I turn to pat him, but the bed is empty where he should be. "Gabe?" I call out terrified that aliens have abducted him when I was fast asleep. It's unlike him to wake up before eight in the morning unless he has class or is writing an exam. “Gabe?” I call out again and jump out of bed, kicking the covers away.

“Hey, I am here.” He calls back from what sounds like the kitchen. Two things are peculiar about this morning: Gabe is awake before me, and he is making breakfast.

“What are you doing?”

“Good morning sleepy-head,” he says sensually, and steals a kiss before I can argue about having not brushed my teeth yet. The kitchen smells of waffles, bacon, and eggs; and I can hear the kettle boiling water for coffee. Who died and turned my boyfriend into Jamie Oliver?

“What happened here?” I ask sleepily and rub my eyes. Maybe I’m still dreaming, I’m definitely not fully awake yet.

“I made breakfast.”

“Why? Who’s coming?”

“No one, it’s just you and me.”

“But babe, you never make breakfast.”

“I do, on your birthday and Valentine’s day.”

“But today is none of those.”

“Can you just appreciate that I am being a very loving boyfriend and stop questioning everything?”

“Okay. Whatever you say, Chef Gabriel. What’s on the menu?” It is hard not to get pulled in when Gabe is excited, and today he is showing all his tell-tales of having the heebie-jeebies. He pushes a plate of mixed fruit in front of me and I smile happily, like a child in a candy shop.

“I want to say thank you for this weekend. It was perfect.”

"Including the almost-dead ex?" I tease, but the experience is not something I'd wish on anyone, friend or foe.

"Especially the almost-dead ex... Do not interrupt my speech. I admire how you handled everything, you do not cease to amaze me and that is why I want you to know that I plan to spend the rest of my existence with you. Come rain or sun I want to be happy with you. Marry me, Zimkhita Zungu. Please?"

Then I see it. The gorgeous stone that would make anyone scream "yes!" without thinking twice is right in front of me.

"Yes." It comes out very soft, even though my heart is blinded by the ring. "Yes."

Chapter 21

Black girls everywhere will know how to forgive themselves

"Hello."

"Hello, may I please speak to Miss Melisa McFarland?"

"This is she."

"Miss McFarland, this is Mina Dohman from the Gemaldegalerie, based in Berlin, Germany."

"Excuse me, you said what?"

"The Gemmal..." but I cut her mid-word with my sudden screaming.

"Oh, my word. Oh, my word." She allows me to have my moment before continuing as poised and as professional as if I have not just damaged her eardrum.

"We received some of your work from one of your professors and we would very much like it if you could come to spend a year interning here at the gallery."

This is the very same gallery that contains artwork from as early as the 13th century, is built above water, and most important is that it houses 16 masterpieces by Rembrandt. If there was a heaven on earth, this would be it. It is every artist's dream to experience the magic found in this place. What a dream it is to be asked to work there as an intern. I could be asked to make tea with no pay and only have the comfort of sleeping under a bridge, and I'd still say yes… a thousand times and over.

"Yes! Yes! You do not even have to ask. Oh, my word."

"Please go to our website and confirm your contact details and we will email you the rest of the information."

"Yes, thank you."

"It's our pleasure, Miss McFarland. Looking forward to hearing from you."

I close my eyes and scream at the top of my lungs before I can hang up the phone. Yes, this is really happening. Me, the girl with the green eyes and curves that can put you in a coma, I am going to Germany, and as frightening as the idea is it couldn't have come at a better time. I do not even have time to think about how my mother is going to feel about it because I already know that she's not ready to have me out of the nest, and definitely not so far away.

Sibahle is going to scream. She has always been the one I share things with, and I'm not entirely sure how the sudden news is going to hit her. I'm not even bothered about Mxo because he knows me only when he wants some money, and Luke (with his wavy blonde hair and enticing green eyes) will simply nod his head and say "rad".

The one wearing bermuda shorts, holding a glass of whiskey… my father, who seems to always have leftover food stuck in his beard, is the one I'll enjoy sharing the news with most. We share a lot… a surname, a love for vintage collectibles, and a true appreciation for art.

While my need to get away as fast as possible could not have come at a worse time, I don't feel guilty for choosing the easy way out, of following my dreams, but I do feel guilty for running away from my reality. I shy away from my father's sad face but must admit the truth to myself.

I have just told him, without first handing him a glass of whisky, that I am leaving for Germany in two days. Yes, I have made up my mind. I'm taking that internship and have already gone through the academic requirements with my professors. I will not have a problem fulfilling the requirements. Depending on how well I do at the Gemaldegalerie, and what wonderful things Miss Mina Dohman will be saying about me, I might not even need to worry about making it to graduation because the very nice people at the Art Department from the University of the Free State have concluded that they would be willing to pass me on merit. Despite the good news, and even though I have a very good chance of doing something amazing for a year, I still feel like I am running away. I feel like this is just an excuse. Like I just got out of a bad relationship and using Germany (and all its glory) as a rebound.

My father, however, does not seem jubilant at the very short notice. "Why so soon?" he asks, his eyes a very cold and empty green, the same as mine, and it is at this moment that I appreciate how very alike we are. I thank him for that.

"Dad I just found out three days ago, and I'm still trying to wrap my head around what is happening myself. It just jumped on me."

"But I know you, Melisa. You have never gone through with things because they just ended up on your lap, why does this have to be different?"

"Daddy, I know this is a shock but it's a worthwhile tremor. I could be famous."

"I do not understand what being famous has to do with it."

"Okay, now you sound like mom. Can't you be happy that your daughter is going to Germany to work at a world-renowned gallery and will be the envy of every prospective artist on this earth? Please... for me."

"I am extremely proud of you, I won't deny that, but I still feel this is too abrupt. Have you even talked to your mother about it?"

"Well... that... is where you come in."

"You mean your mother doesn't know about this? Melisa, what is going on with you?"

"Dad, you and I both know that it's not easy having a conversation with that woman. I mean I'm 22, but she still treats me like I am 12. This would start a war, and I love her too much to watch as her heart broke."

"And how exactly are you expecting to let her know?"

"I was hoping you'd do it," I say with a sweet sly smile, but my father returns a quick growl. "No!" he snaps and I have to raise my eyebrows to make sure I heard him well.

"No!" he says again, louder this time, so I have no excuse for not hearing him. "You are running away from something Melisa, or someone, and I'm not going to be a part of that," and the look in his eyes tells me that he is not backing down.

He looks like a dog with a bone, and he's not letting go of his prize. In my 22 years of living, I've learned when to stand my ground, when to hide, when to make known how I feel, when to roll my eyes at my mother (which is only permissible when she is not watching), but definitely when to tell my father the truth.

Today, by far one of the best days of my life, was not when I would unlearn that.

"It is someone, Daddy, but I'm okay. I just need a fresh start, and this is it," I whisper, hoping to convince him, but knowing full well that I am the one that most needs to believe it. I went to the Eastern Cape, going after a guy I had fallen for when I wasn't even trying to, once upon a time. I loved him from a distance until I felt confident enough to tell him how I felt, but that's the problem with being too honest with people, you end up believing that they would return the favor, and that you can come back from it from the shock.

Sabelo with skin the color of raisins and a beautiful white smile made me a believer in love. He had charmed his way into my heart in the sneakiest way possible and I did not blame him. He was smart, educated, came from a good home, and had morals (something not many people my age could proudly say they possessed).

I mean isn't this what girls are taught to look for in a man? The security of a steady check, a comfortable dwelling, and the assurance that you scored big? What they just don't tell you is that he could have someone who, no matter how mean she is, is still his fiancée and the mother of his unborn child. It still hurt a lot to just think about how the conversation went after declaring our love for each other. I was still drunk from his kisses, mesmerized by his soulful eyes, when he stood back and cleared his throat.

"I first have to tell you something," he said, and I immediately knew that I did not like the tone of his voice and that I would not like what he would say next.

"I know, my mom is going to go crazy, but I'll tell her that I love you."

"No, I love you, Melissa. I've always loved you," he continued, all the while melting my heart and breaking down all the walls I had built. He reminded me of a Von Gogh painting that I had come across but failed to acknowledge its raw detail because I was busy with other things. How could this beautiful mortal love me so hard that I felt his heartbeat every time he said my name?

"I love you Melissa, but I cannot leave with you... not right now."

"Why?"

"Because Chichi is pregnant."

Those words felt like a slap to my face. He did not need to claim the child as his for me to understand that he was not that type of a man. Not the type to leave behind a pregnant woman he was not in love with for someone who touched him like the ink on her hands could never dry... looked at him with eyes that had never really seen anyone but him... loved him like a hurricane, and was even prepared to open herself up to him like it was the only thing she knew how to do.

That he was not that type of a man, made me hate him more and hate myself too for wanting such evilness. It was the reason that I had to leave, and leave now. It was also why I prayed that I could eventually forgive myself for everything that I felt. Someday... it didn't have to be at that moment.

Printed in the United States
by Baker & Taylor Publisher Services